# Treasure
# On
# Chincoteague
# Island

*Written and Illustrated*
*by*
*Karen Simpson-Tweedie*

Carolyn an
Bill,

Beware of
pirates!

Karen

*To my parents, Pat and Richard,*
*my lifelong teachers of life and love.*
*And to the Davids in my life:*
*My brother, my mentor, my friend;*
*My husband, my partner, the love of my life.*
*Our adventure of life continues!*

Thanks to Ron Peek of Treasures of Maryland for his invaluable
help with coins; to Linda Murphy of Eastbay Advertising for her
photography and general handholding; to Shannon Barbour for her
pony expertise; to Regina Belote for her assistance with local setting
details; to Michael Stephano for generous technical support; and to
my Sheepdog Press family: Nelly, who guides me from above, and
Daisy, my new publisher in training.

SHEEPDOG PRESS

"Woof!"

Published by
Sheepdog Press
P.O. Box 60
Onancock, Virginia 23417
www.sheepdogpress.com

Library of Congress Control Number: 2003093989
ISBN 0-9742205-0-7
Printed in the United States of America

Cover painting, "Chincoteague", by the author.

# CONTENTS

# Chapter 1

# The Island

The young girl was packing clothes into her duffle bag. She carefully considered each item as she took it from the drawer and placed it in the bag. In went her bathing suit, then another, along with plenty of shorts and tee shirts. She pulled her sweatshirt out the of drawer, started to place it on top of the pile of clothes in the bag, then reconsidered and put it back. No, she thought, I don't need this. It's going to be hot at the beach and I won't need it at all. The weather's so different here in Virginia. Back home, when she went to the beach with her parents, she always needed a sweatshirt. But she was learning that the Eastern Shore was very different from her home on the west coast near San Francisco.

When she was satisfied that all the necessary clothes were packed, she hopped onto the patchwork quilt covering her old oak bed and picked up a small book that was laying beside her duffle bag. It seemed that she had been doing a lot of packing lately. Just a month before, she had packed her bags to spend her summer vacation with her grandparents at their summer home in Accomac, Virginia, all the way across the country from her home with her parents. She thought she would have her grandparents to herself, but then her cousin, a girl about her age, had arrived for the summer, too. But now the girls were leaving to spend some time with the family of another cousin, Jack, a cousin they hadn't even met until a few weeks ago. The girls' grandparents would join them in a few days for a big family get together. For an only child, she was suddenly surrounded by family.

She ran her hand across the dark red leather cover of the book, then unwound the tie that held the book closed. This book was very special to her. It had been a gift from her mother last week when her parents surprised her with a visit, given to her just before the girl's mother and father had returned home. It had a grown-up look and feel that was enchanting. The leather smelled wonderful, like her mother's new leather purse and the leather seats inside her parents' new car. There was a long, thin loop that held a new pen close to the gold edges of the book's pages. She carefully opened the cover, still stiff with newness, and retrieved a folded newspaper clipping that was tucked between the marbled pages of the inner cover. Morning sun streamed through the wavy glass in the old windows and glistened off her long, silky brown hair as she slowly unfolded the paper. She read the article carefully. She could almost recite it from memory, she had read it so many times in the past two weeks.

### Local Children Uncover Secrets from the Past:
### A Secret Diary

Megan Brown and her cousin, Kendall Scott, granddaughters of Warren and Elizabeth Bayley of Accomac, made a series of unique discoveries this summer while vacationing on the Eastern Shore. The cousins purchased a box at a local auction that held many valuable antiques from the early 1800s. Among their treasures were a sampler, a silver spoon given by Agnes Kerr in 1809, and several wonderfully preserved letters written in 1809 and 1810.

The girls also discovered a diary that had been hidden away for nearly 200 years. The diary contained valuable information identifying an important early joiner, or carpenter, a man named Edwin Matthews.

In addition to learning the name of that joiner, the girls, along with their cousin, Jack Walker, of Accomac, unearthed a collection of antique wooden molding planes believed to have once belonged to Edwin Matthews.

Along with the planes, the children discovered a first edition of the extremely rare architectural resource, "Palladio Londinensis; or, The London Art of Building", which was published in 1734. This book is one of only seven first edition copies know in existence in the world. It was found in a secret compartment in an abandoned cottage on the Bayley's property.

Further research into the discoveries made by these children has led to the identity of two early decoy carvers: Daniel Edmonds and Joshua Walker, both now known to be distant relatives of Jack Walker.

This very important collection of early local artifacts is on loan to the Eastern Shore of Virginia Historical Society and will be on display at Kerr Place in Onancock for the remainder of this year. After that, the collection will join other significant artifacts as part of a large, early American history exhibit that will be touring the United States for two years.

Brown, Scott, and Walker are collaborating on a children's book about their adventures. They are being assisted by Miss Brown's mother, well known mystery writer, Rachel Brown, daughter of the Bayleys.

The sound of rapid footsteps on the stairs interrupted the girl's thoughts. "Are you ready, Megan? asked the taller girl as she entered the bedroom.

"Almost," Megan answered as she quickly folded the newspaper article and placed it back into its safe place inside the red book and dropped it down inside her bag. "I just have to make sure I have everything, then I'll be ready." She looked up at her cousin. "Are you packed?"

"Yeah! I already have my bag on the porch. Jack just called and their van's packed. They're ready to go as soon as we are." The girl glanced around Megan's room. "Don't worry about forgetting anything. Grandma and Grandpa will be coming up in a few days, so they can bring anything you forgot," assured Kendall breathlessly. "Grandma has a big cooler downstairs for us, filled with food. Mrs. Walker that, I know. Hurry up, Meg, and meet me I can't wait to get going," Kendall said ove der as she quickly headed back down the stairs.

Megan took a final look around her cozy little room and her eyes rested on the lovely old rag doll resting comfortably in a small chair. She smiled and shook her head in silent amazement at all that had happened in such a short time. Why, only a month before she'd been in tears at the thought of spending the summer with her grandparents, so far away from home. Now she was pleased that she would be here for another month, but somewhat nervous about spending the next few days with strangers. "Okay, Nelly, you can come, too," she said as she carefully picked up the homespun doll and tenderly placed her on the bed. A familiar face in the room she would share with Kendall might be comforting, even if it is just a rag doll. At the last minute she changed her mind once again and retrieved her sweatshirt from the dresser drawer, wrapped it around the precious doll, and settled them both into her duffle bag. She zipped it closed and hoisted the large bag up on her shoulder and headed out the door with one last glance around her room.

"Kendall has money in case you girls need anything before we get up to Chincoteague," Grandpa explained to Megan as they assembled bags, beach towels, and a large cooler on the front porch. He said the name of the island with a soft *sh* sound, different than one might think to pronounce it when reading the word. Grandpa had explained that it was another of the many Indian names found on the Shore, like Wachapreague and Pungoteague, Machipongo and Assateague. "You'll stay with Jack's aunt and uncle in town for a few days, then you girls can come and join us at the campground if you want. Don't worry, we'll be there in plenty of time for

Pony Penning." The girls knew that Grandma was tired from all the company they had had since the girls' now-famous discoveries and was looking forward to a few days of rest before going up to Chincoteague Island.

So much was happening, Megan didn't know how to react to it all. After learning that they were distant cousins, Jack's mother had practically adopted the girls and then invited them to join their family up on Chincoteague for the festivities surrounding the annual pony roundup called Pony Penning. Megan knew that there was a pony swim and a carnival and crowds of people and was flattered to be invited, but didn't know Jack or the Walker family all that well. Kendall had jumped at the idea and Megan hadn't told anyone of her hesitation about going. Another family had offered Grandma and Grandpa the use of their RV that was parked at a campground on Chincoteague. Kendall's parents had just left two days ago to return to New Hampshire and it had been fun visiting with them. Megan's parents had been there for several days about a week earlier and she had enjoyed showing them around town, even though her parents had spent their childhood summers there. Both girls' parents had been in town when the cousins, including Jack, had generously loaned all of their treasures to Kerr Place, the museum in Onancock, the next town over. Well, everything except the old homespun rag doll. Megan wanted to keep her and Kendall had agreed, since Megan was the one who found the hidden key that unlocked the rest of the mystery.

When the girls accompanied Grandma to Food Lion to grocery shop, it took them an extra hour because of all the people who wanted to stop and visit with them. They all knew about Megan's and Kendall's disc

and treated the cousins as celebrities. It seemed that everyone was related to each other or at least knew everyone else, something she remembered her mother telling
her about the Eastern Shore. But her mother had also
described it as a quiet place, slow paced, that time had
just about forgotten. This whirlwind of activity sure
didn't feel slow paced to Megan. Maybe it would be
different when they got to the island.

"You'll have a great time with the Walkers. Jack's
Aunt Pat and Uncle Rich are wonderful folks. They'll
take good care of you girls and we'll be up in a few
days," assured Grandma as she joined them on the
porch and gave Megan a warm hug. She surveyed the
girls' belongings. "Looks like you have everything you
need."

"Here they come!" exclaimed Kendall as the
Walker's van appeared. After a minute or two of hugs
and good-byes, the van was packed and the girls joined
the Walker family, leaving Grandma and Grandpa smiling and waving on the front porch.

Megan sat quietly and watched out the van window
as they rode along windy country roads headed for
Chincoteague Island. Kendall was chattering excitedly
with Jack and his parents. Megan saw rows of small
houses pass by, with people sitting out front under
shady old trees, trying to stay cool in the summer heat.
Here and there she saw children playing, a woman
hanging laundry on a line to dry, people working in
their vegetable gardens and on larger farms, and old
folks sitting, fanning themselves. Then they passed a
tiny white church with a small cemetery nearby. And
everywhere it was green. The trees were green, the

lawns were green, the farm fields were green. It seemed like everything was growing and flourishing.

Back in California, in the heat of the summer, the hills were all dried to a familiar brownish gold. It rarely rained there in the summer, so unless people watered their yards, everything seemed pretty dry. It was refreshing to see so much life. Megan had already experienced a few of the Eastern Shore's summer rains since her arrival a month ago. She had never seen so much rain come down so hard, so fast, and the accompanying lightning and thunder were dramatic and exciting. Sometimes it even poured rain while the sun was still shining. Grandpa called those "sun showers". During summer rains, the streets became rivers within minutes, but because it was warm outside, you could sit on the front porch and watch the action. Then, the rain would stop, the sun would come out, and there would be a delicious smell of wet leaves and grass all around.

"Megan, how did it go with your mom?" asked Mrs. Walker, interrupting her reverie. "Did she get all information she needs for the book?"

"Yes, she asked us a lot of questions and taped it all. We told her everything we could remember, right, Kendall?"

"Oh, we told her every little thing we could think of. She said she'll call when she has more questions, and she gave Megan a book to write stuff in, if we think of anything we forgot to tell her. She talked to you, too, didn't she, Jack?" Kendall asked.

"Yes. She thought the stuff about finding that old architecture book behind the secret door was pretty cool." He turned to face Megan. "You think she'll really write a book about us?" he asked.

"Well, she said she's going to. She finished the book she was working on, her next mystery, so she has some time to write it. She usually writes two books or so a year and isn't ready to start the next one yet. She said she has a lot of research to do for the next book and would like to do something different for a few months. She was really excited about the stuff we found. She said we had 'an adventure worthy of telling', or something like that. Anyway, she even called her editor and told him about it. He liked the idea too."

"Maybe they'll make a movie about us," offered Kendall.

"Get real!" scoffed Jack.

"Hey, Jack, what's that place?" Megan asked as they passed by a big yellow and red building with a huge American flag waving in the breeze out front and a sign proclaiming it "The Dream".

"Oh, The Dream. That's a roller skating rink. It's a pretty cool place. Brian and I like to go there sometimes. They have great pizza!"

"And when we were your age, we went there, too," Mrs. Walker said. "It's been here for ages, for over 50 years, and it's still owned by the same family that started it, the Justice family."

"That's right," Mr. Walker continued. "The grandson of the original owner runs it now, along with his sons. I believe it started out as a restaurant with car hops on roller skates coming out to the cars to take orders."

"Really? The waitresses were on skates?" Megan asked.

"That's what I hear. Then, they built a second building with the roller rink inside and connected it to the restaurant. We thought you kids might like to go there one day next week," said Mr. Walker. "Do you girls know how to skate?"

"Yes, I do," answered Megan.

"Me, too!" Kendall said.

"Great. Then we'll all go up there one day. That'll be fun."

"Too bad Brian isn't here. It'd be more fun, but he's at camp," Jack said.

"Hey, what's that?" Megan asked, pointing toward a large fenced area filled with huge satellite dishes aimed at the sky.

"That's the NASA Wallops Flight Facility. They build and test satellites here. Can you see those rockets over there? They have launches here sometimes, and do a lot of space research. We know several people on the Shore who work at Wallops."

"Cool!" said Kendall. "Are there astronauts here?"

"No, they launch only unmanned rockets here, for research, although I understand that years ago they sent up some rockets with chimpanzees in them."

"Monkey astronauts? Awesome," Jack said.

A short time later, the van was headed across the Chincoteague causeway, a narrow two-lane road surrounded on either side by marshland as far as the eye could see. Tapered streams of shallow water branched this way and that, then widened, then narrowed again, in a seemingly endless maze of little rivers. Tall grasses edged the streams and funny birds perched on the grass or stood knee deep in the water, waiting for lunch to swim by. Ahead was the tiny drawbridge, the only entrance to Chincoteague Island.

At the foot of the bridge was Main Street, a busy array of shops, houses, cars, and lots of people. "How come there are so many people here?" asked Kendall as she watched the traffic move slowly along Main Street.

"Honey, it's Pony Penning time," answered Mrs. Walker. "People come from all over the country for Pony Penning. Everybody loves to see the ponies swim over from Assateague, and lots of people come to try to buy a pony at the auction." She pointed to shop windows plastered with posters of horses. "Don't worry, you'll catch pony fever just like the rest of us," she explained with a smile.

"Yes, it's nuts around here in July. It's always busy in the summer because people come to the beach, but we really pack them in for the pony swim and carnival and stuff. It's really fun. I come every year," Jack said.

They turned off Main Street and drove past several blocks of small houses spaced closely together. "Here we are," announced Mr. Walker as he pulled the van into the driveway of a neat yellow house.

"We're here!" chimed the girls.

"Oh, and Jack, we have a little surprise waiting for you in Aunt Pat's house," said Mr. Walker.

"Honey, his surprise isn't little at all," corrected Mrs. Walker with a sly smile.

## CHAPTER 2

# JACK'S SURPRISE

∿ᴑℓ᠘ᘯ◯◯◯ᘖ᠘ᕷᕵᘖᗞ◯⊖

"Jack, help me unload these bags, will you?" asked Mr. Walker. As they climbed out of the van they were greeted by their hosts, Jack's aunt and uncle.

"Welcome! We're so glad you could come and stay with us. I've heard so much about you two," said Aunt Pat to the girls. "You must be Kendall," she said as she gave Kendall a warm hug. "And you're little Megan." She hugged Megan and patted her on the shoulder. "I'm Pat Kellam, and this is my husband, Rich." The man with her smiled at the girls as he started to carry several bags into the house. "You girls are family, so please call us Aunt Pat and Uncle Rich." Aunt Pat waved to the teenage girl who was coming out of the house next door. "Ashley, come on over and meet the girls."

An athletic looking sandy-haired girl skirted around the bushes that divided the two driveways. "Hi, I'm Ashley James. I read all about you two in the newspaper. You've had quite an adventure this summer, huh?"

"Yeah, it's been interesting, that's for sure," said Kendall. "I'm Kendall Scott and this is my cousin, Megan Brown."

"Hi," Megan said.

"Well, I'm off to work, but it's nice to meet you guys. I work at Muller's, it's an ice cream store downtown, so come on in sometime and we can get to know each

other, okay?" Ashley smiled at the girls, and waved to
Jack as she climbed into her red pickup truck. "Hey
there, Jack. Congratulations on making it into the paper! See you later," she called.

"Ice cream sounds good to me," said an unfamiliar
voice from behind Aunt Pat. The girls turned to see
who it was as Jack shouted, "Brian!"

A boy with spiked blond hair who appeared to be
the same age as Jack stepped out from where he was
hiding. "Hey, man, how you doing?"

"Brian, I thought you were at camp." Jack now noticed a bright orange cast on Brian's left arm. "What
happened to you?"

"Camp was sweet, man, totally cool, but I had a little
accident. I was demonstrating our famous double
skateboard flip off a picnic table and didn't quite nail
the landing. Broke my wing!" He pointed to his left
arm, completely encased in a cast to his shoulder.
"Check it out. The orange is pretty cool, don't you
think?"

"Yeah, but doesn't it hurt? And when did this happen?" He turned to his mother. "Mom, how come you
didn't tell me that Brian got hurt?"

"Brian thought it would be fun to surprise you,
honey," answered Mrs. Walker. "His mother and Aunt
Pat are good friends and Aunt Pat invited Brian to stay
here, too. So, are you surprised?" she asked.

"Totally." Jack turned back to Brian. "Hey, man,
these are my new cousins, Megan and Kendall. They're
here for Pony Penning."

Brian nodded his greeting to the girls. "I read all
about you guys in the newspaper. I'm Brian Belote,
Jack's best bud. All that stuff you found is pretty cool.

And you're all cousins. Amazing. Everybody's a cousin around here. Listen, Jack," he said as he turned to face his friend, lowering his voice. "I've been reading some stuff since I broke my arm and we have some serious work to do."

"Work? What are you talking about?"

"Pirates, man, I'm talking about pirates."

14

## CHAPTER 3

## PIRATES

The boys were huddled over the stack of books and papers that had been unceremoniously pulled from Brian's backpack. They had gotten settled into their room, had enjoyed a delicious dinner topped off with homemade brownies all from Grandma Bayley's cooler,
and were sitting outside in the backyard. Jack was listening intently as Brian described the pirate quest.

"I guess it started with 'Treasure Island'. I read it at camp a few weeks ago. A kid from Richmond said he'd read it and it was really cool, so I borrowed it from the camp library. Then one of the counselors at camp told us there's an exhibit of some real pirate treasure coins here on Chincoteague this summer, gold doubloons, really old silver coins, cool old stuff from actual shipwrecks. And there's one coin called the Knight Rider. I've got to see that. There was an article in the Eastern Shore News all about it. After I broke my arm, I couldn't do too much at camp, so that same counselor went to the library in Accomac and got me a bunch of books about pirates. He thought it would keep me busy since I couldn't play ball or canoe or stuff like that. Well, I was reading some of it and you won't believe what I found out."

"What?" Jack asked.

"Well, there were plenty of pirates, real pirates, right here on Chincoteague, a couple of hundred years ago!"

"Are you kidding? Here? Come on, Brian, there weren't pirates on Chincoteague. Just a bunch of old horses were here."

"Oh, yeah? Well, check this out, man," he said as he reached for one of the books from the pile. " 'To My Brother, George Wilson,' " he read. " 'There are three creeks lying 100 paces or more north of the second inlet above Chincoteague Island, Virginia, which is at the southward end of the peninsula. At the head of the third creek to the northward is a bluff facing the Atlantic Ocean with three cedar trees growing on it, each about 1 1/2 yards apart. Between the trees I buried ten iron bound chests, bars of silver, gold, diamonds and jewels to the sum of 200,000 pounds sterling. Go to the woody knoll secretly and remove the treasure.' Do you get what this is, Jack? This letter was written around 1750 by a guy from South Carolina named Charles Wilson. He was a pirate and was caught and put in prison in England waiting to be hanged, and he wanted his brother to go find his treasure. But from what I've read, this letter was discovered about 200 years after it was written and his brother never got it. And since the letter was found, lots of people have looked for the treasure but no one has found it yet."

"That's pretty cool," Jack said. "So there's a real pirate treasure buried here on Chincoteague?"

"Yes, with ten chests of gold and stuff, and we're going to find it, Jack. Just you and me, man."

"How are we going to do that?" Jack asked. "What the heck do we know about finding pirate treasures?"

"I have some ideas, some plans, but we're going to have to be careful so that no one else finds out what we're doing. I don't want anyone else to get to the treasure before we do."

"Well, maybe Megan and Kendall could help, too."

"No way, man, this is a guy thing, just you and me. We don't need any girls around to mess things up.

"They aren't like that, Brian, really. They're pretty cool, for girls," Jack said.

"Pirate stuff is guy stuff, okay? Let's keep it that way, Jack. Besides, what would girls want to know about pirates," Brian said.

"Pirates? Did you say something about pirates?" asked Kendall as she and Megan joined the boys outside.

Brian quickly closed the book with the Charles Wilson letter and slid it into his backpack. "I was just telling Jack about some books I was reading at camp. Books about pirates."

"Oh, so what did you read?" Kendall asked as she sat down and looked over the pile of books on the table.

"First I read 'Treasure Island'. Ever hear of it?"

"Yeah, I read it last year. What else do you have here?" she asked, reaching for one of the books.

"I found out some pretty cool stuff about pirates." He reached for another book and flipped open the front cover. "This one was first written in 1724."

"1724? Wait a minute," Jack said. He turned to Kendall. "When was our book written, the one we found in the cupboard? Wasn't that 1724 too?"

"No, ours was written in 1734, ten years later," answered Kendall.

"Brian, that book's really old. Where did you get

it?" Jack asked.

"It isn't mine; it's from the library. And this is just a copy, printed later, but it's the same as the old one. It even has some pretty awesome old drawings in it of pirates and their ships. It's all about a bunch of pirates and each chapter is about a different pirate and tells all about what they did, treasures they stole, and most of the time, about how they were caught and killed. Lots of times they were hanged or got their heads cut off. Sometimes the pirates were called buccaneers or freebooters, but I like the word pirate the best. It has a cool ring to it."

Megan turned to Brian. "Is that really true? I mean, were there really pirates and treasures and stuff? I thought that was just pretend like in Peter Pan. I didn't know there were really pirates a long time ago."

"Oh, yeah, you'd be surprised about what those guys did. They were really bad, I mean really bad. And they double crossed each other all the time. They looked for ships that weren't very well armed or protected, then just got on board, killed the guys on the ship, and stole everything they could. They'd even take the food and water so they had it for their ship." Kendall, Jack, and even Megan were all interested and encouraged Brian to tell them more. "There was this one English guy named Avery. He was the first mate on a big ship. Then he got a bunch of the crew together and he took over the ship and became the new captain and sent the old captain back to land in a little boat. They sailed around and found two other smaller boats and those guys joined up with Avery, too. Then he and the guys in the other two boats starting robbing stuff from other ships, like gold and anything valuable. Once they stole a huge load of gold and diamonds from a ship with a king's daughter on it. Then, Avery got the captains of the two smaller pirate ships to put all the treasures on his ship because his was much bigger and he could keep it all safe. Of course, after all the stuff was on his ship, he and his guys left in the middle of the night and stole all jewels!"

"What a creep! He tricked his own friends," Kendall said.

"They weren't friends, that's for sure. All those guys were pretty rotten dudes. But you have to hear the end of the story," Brian continued. "Most of Avery's guys took their share of gold and settled in America. But Avery went back to England. He had gold but he also had a huge bunch of diamonds. You see, the dude had kept the most valuable part of the treasure hidden even from his own men. But he couldn't sell the diamonds without people getting suspicious, like, where would he have all of a sudden gotten so many diamonds, so he used a friend who had connections with a bunch of wealthy merchants who could sell the diamonds for him. Avery had to give all his diamonds to the merchants and he waited for his money. The funny thing is, they double crossed him, and he ended up with nothing."

"Served him right, the greedy creep!" Kendall said.

"Yeah, I'd sure hate to run across someone like that," Megan said.

"The thing is, no one could trust any one. All the pirates were only out for themselves."

"Where did the pirates come from? Why were those guys being pirates and taking stuff?" Megan asked.

"Well, some of them were rotten guys, criminals

who just liked stealing, I guess. And some were run-
away servants who were trying to get rich, and some
were just young guys who were looking for adventure.
Some of the pirates were pretty young, just teenagers,
and lots of them got killed. But some of them got really
rich and then moved some place and had a big pile of
gold to live off of for the rest of their lives. People
heard stories about some guys getting rich and wanted
to do the same thing. I guess that happens now, too.
You know, some people do scams to get rich and it usually hurts somebody else, and most of the time the scam
backfires. But people keep trying."

"What else did you find out about pirates?" Kendall
asked.

"I read this other thing about a guy named Thomas
Beale who buried his treasure someplace in Virginia,
then wrote letters in code that tell where it's buried. He
and a group of 30 other guys mined a huge amount of
gold and silver somewhere near Santa Fe. Then they
figured they needed to put it in some kind of a safe
place, so Beale and some of the guys brought it to Virginia in several loads and found a really safe place to
hid it. The men were afraid that if something happened
to all of them, their relatives would never be able to find
the treasure, it was so well hidden. So Beale gave a letter to a man he trusted in Virginia describing how he
had discovered the gold and silver and that the treasure
was to be divided up into 31 shares for the relatives of
the 31 men who mined it. Then there were three more
letters written in a number code that gave the exact lo-
cation of the treasure, details about how much gold and
silver was buried there, and who the people were who
would get the 31 shares. Beale put those letters in a

locked box and gave them to the man and told him not to open it for about 10 or 15 years. Beale was supposed to send the man a final letter telling him how to figure out the code, but that letter never arrived. People have been trying to figure out his secret code for over 175 years and no one has cracked it yet." He showed them several pages in one of the books that were covered with rows and rows of numbers. "That's the code, these numbers. No one's figured it out yet." He looked up at Jack and the girls. "Maybe we could make up our own code. What do you think?"

"That sounds fun," Megan said. "Maybe we could bury our own treasure and write clues in our code to find it, or maybe make a treasure map."

"Yeah, maybe Megan and I could hide something from you two, and you guys could hide something from us, and then we can all have a treasure hunt," Kendall said.

Brian thought for a moment and realized that would play right into his plan. "Awesome idea. You like the idea, Jack?" Brian asked his friend with a wink.

"Yeah, very cool. I really like the idea of having our own code. That's sweet."

"Now, to get us in the true pirate mood, I'll tell you about the worst guy ever, Blackbeard!" Brian said.

"How are you kids doing out here?" asked Mrs. Walker as she came out the back door. The screen door closed behind her with a smack. "Want more brownies? We have plenty. Your grandmother was so sweet to send all this food," she said, smiling at the girls. She noticed the books piled on the table in front of the children and spoke to the boys. "Pirates? You're reading about pirates?"

"Yeah, Mom, Brian read a bunch of books about pirates when he was at camp and he's telling us all about them."

"That's interesting." She turned to Brian. "Did you know there are some real treasure coins on display over at the Chamber of Commerce building? We'll have to go see them while the girls are here."

"Yes, ma'am. Told you, man," Brian said to Jack. "Yes, I read about them in the newspaper. That would be awesome, Mrs. W. I'd really like to check them out."

"Well, you kids have fun," Mrs. Walker said as she went back inside.

Brian picked up one of the books, flipped through many pages until he came to the part he wanted to read aloud. "Listen to this. 'With the name of pirate is also associated ideas of rich plunder, caskets of buried jewels, chests of gold ingots, bags of outlandish coins, secreted in lonely, out of the way places, or buried about the wild shores of rivers, and unexplored sea coasts, near rocks and trees bearing mysterious marks, indicating where the treasure was hid. And as it is his invariable practice to secrete and bury his booty, and from the perilous life he leads, being often killed or captured, he can never revisit the spot again; immense sums remain buried in those places, and are irrecoverably lost.' " Brian closed the book he was reading from. "This means that the pirates stole jewels, gold, and bags of coins, and buried them near the coast, near special trees or rocks so they could find them later. But since they were usually killed, they never went back to where they hid their treasures. So there's probably a lot of treasure hidden all over, especially near the water," Brian said, and again winked at Jack.

"What does 'booty' mean, Brian?" Kendall asked.

"It's the treasure the pirates stole. There are some other pirate words I learned, too, like marooning. If the pirates wanted to get rid of some guy but didn't want to kill him, they would put him onto an island, usually some little deserted island, and leave him there to make it on his own. That was marooning. And the black flag that pirates flew on their ships that had a skull and bones on it was called a roger. Each pirate made up his own flag design and flew it on his ship. Sometimes the skulls look like they're smiling, so maybe that's why they called them jolly rogers, but I'm not sure.

"So, you were going to tell us about that guy, Black-beard. Was he a pirate, too?" asked Kendall.

"That dude was one tough guy. He was big and mean. And he had a bushy, black beard, which is why he was called Blackbeard. His real name was Edward Teach. He was another English guy, but he came to America and was doing a lot of pirating in the Atlantic Ocean. In fact, he had this ship called Revenge, and he used Assateague Island as one of his hideouts. And so did that guy, Charles Wilson, the one I told you about before."

"Charles Wilson? You didn't say anything about him before," interrupted Kendall.

"Oh, I guess I was telling Jack about him before." Brian flashed Jack a quick look, then continued. "Well, he wasn't as interesting as Blackbeard. Anyway, Black-beard somehow became friends with the Governor of North Carolina and the Governor got a cut of the stuff he stole, his booty, so the Governor let him do his thing. Well, this big dude tried to look as mean as he could, and used to twist his long beard into tails and tie stuff around them and tuck some of them over his ears."

"That's creepy," said Megan.

"Yeah, and he had all kinds of pistols hanging from holsters around him and stuck lighted matches around the edge of his hat, burning matches, so that he would look tough. Can you imagine?"

"I'd hate to meet that guy in a dark alley," laughed Jack.

"No kidding. And when the Governor of Virginia was sick of hearing all this stuff that Blackbeard was doing, he sent one of his lieutenants with a bunch of his guys to get him. There was a huge battle on the water and Blackbeard got on the lieutenant's ship and they looked at each other eyeball to eyeball. Then they started shooting and stabbing each other and finally Blackbeard fell over dead. It took five bullet holes and 20 stab wounds to finally kill him. That's how tough he was. And the lieutenant cut off Blackbeard's head and put it on the front of his ship and sailed back to Virginia to show the Governor."

"Okay, that's too gross. That's enough pirates for me. How am I supposed to sleep now after hearing all that scary stuff?" Megan asked.

Kendall laughed. "It's okay, Meg. All that happened a long, time ago. There aren't any pirates any more, so stop worrying. Besides, we have plenty to do to keep us busy and keep our minds off of pirates, right?" she said, looking at Jack.

"Yeah, Mom said that we can go skating tomorrow night if we want." He turned to his friend with the orange cast. "Can you skate with that thing, Brian?"

"No way. If I fall again, the doctor said it could make it worse. But I can go with you and hang out."

"Cool. Well, we better go inside and hit the sack, before we get in trouble. Mom and Aunt Pat don't want us staying up too late."

"So, tell me more about this pirate treasure you were talking about before, Brian. How are we supposed to be able to find it if lots of other people have been looking for it for years, and they haven't found it?"

"We have to think like pirates, Jack, and try to figure out where Wilson would have hidden his treasure. With Pony Penning next week, everyone will be busy with all that stuff and no one will even notice what we're doing. We'll have to be cool about it, though, so nobody catches on to what we're up to."

"But why can't we tell Megan and Kendall about it? It might be more fun if they help, too."

"No way, my man. Girls will just slow us down and they could cause all kinds of problems for us. And you see how scared Megan was just talking about pirates? They'd probably end up telling your parents and your aunt and uncle, and then my mom would find out, and she wouldn't be too happy about that."

"Why not? What's the big deal if we start digging around for a treasure? Why would anyone else even care?" Jack asked.

"Because what I didn't tell you is that some people who have looked for buried treasures have gotten hurt, and my mom would go psycho if something else happened to me this summer. She went nuts when I broke my arm, and she'd worry that somehow I'd get hurt again." He noticed a concerned look on Jack's face. "Don't worry, man, we aren't going to get hurt or anything. It's going to be cool. It's just that my mom wor-

ries about me all the time. You know how mothers
are." Brian thought about the girls again. "They can
help us, in a way, Megan and Kendall. We can play pirates with them, you know, the buried treasure hunt we
were talking about, and while they're busy with that,
we can find time to look for Wilson's treasure. It'd be
awesome to find a pirate's treasure, don't you think?
We'd be rich!"

The boys got into their beds and turned out the
lights. "Our pirate quest begins in the morning," Brian
said.

"Cool. Good night, Bri." Jack listened as his friend's
breathing became even. Soon, Brian was fast asleep.
Jack thought about the pirate quest Brian had planned
for them. He still wasn't convinced that they should
keep it a secret from the girls. After all, Megan and
Kendall were his cousins, and the three of them had just
had a rather important adventure of their own. Maybe
Brian was jealous of the notoriety Jack and the girls had
gotten in the newspaper. It seemed that Brian was always telling Jack what to do, making all the plans, calling all the shots. But Brian did have good ideas, and
this Wilson treasure sure did sound exciting. Anyway,
he'd known Brian all his life, and they were best friends,
and Jack had only met the girls a few weeks ago. And
they didn't even know they were cousins until recently.
But that was another story. The girls would be gone at
the end of the summer, and he and Brian would con-
tinue doing what best friends do - hanging out together,
skateboarding, practicing their guitar and drums for
their garage band, Weasels on Skateboards. But with
Brian's arm in a cast, their band would have to wait
while the drummer's arm healed. Well, there were

plenty of other things to do to keep them busy.

Jack wasn't surprised that Brian had read those pirate books. Brian liked to read and that's where he came up with lots of his ideas. Jack didn't read much, only what he had to read for school. His mother was always trying to get him interested in reading books for fun, but Jack could always find something else to do that was more fun. Now that she had seen Brian with his stack of pirate books, she'd probably be expecting Jack to read some of them, too. Great. Jack would rather go crabbing. In fact, he was thinking about getting a new net so that he and Brian could do some crabbing while they were here on Chincoteague. Yes, crabbing sounded fun. Nearly as much fun as a buried treasure.

"Kendall, do you believe all that stuff Brian was telling us about pirates?" Megan asked.

Kendall was in bed propped up on her elbows, watching Megan put her clothes away in the narrow room they shared. "Sure, I believe him. He found all that stuff in that old book that was written in the 1700s when the pirates were still alive. That book was written before our book was, and I thought ours was so old. I never knew there were books that old before this summer, did you? I think it's kind of neat, and I love that we're going to play buried treasure. This could be fun, don't you think, Meg?"

"Well, I like the idea of secret codes and treasures, but those pirates give me the creeps."

"Yeah, I know what you mean. But don't think about that. Boys love that kind of stuff, I guess. My brothers would go nuts over it. Tomorrow night we're going skating, and I want to find out more about this Pony Penning thing. Aunt Pat said there's a carnival this weekend and next week's the auction. I can't wait to see all the horses. I love horses. They're so beautiful. How about you? Do you like horses?"

Megan climbed up onto the top bunk. "I love horses, too, but I've never ridden one. Have you?"

"No, I haven't either, but I wish I could sometime. I can't wait to see the horses up close. Aunt Pat said we'll be able to see them and even pet some of them, maybe."

"Oh, I hope so. That would be so neat." Megan leaned down and hung her head over the side of her bunk so that she could see her cousin. "Can you believe we'll be going to another auction? You know what happened last time we went to an auction," she said with a smile.

"Yeah, it started us on our big adventure of the summer, but this time, we'll just be watching. And besides, it's a pony auction and I'm not planning on buying a pony. It wouldn't fit on the plane!" Kendall thought for a moment about all that the girls had done since they arrived on the Eastern Shore. "We've had enough adventure for one summer, don't you think?"

"No kidding. I'm ready to go to the beach, go skating, eat ice cream, and see lots of horses," Megan said.

"Me, too. Hey, tomorrow let's walk down to the ice cream store where Ashley works and get a cone. Want to?"

"Sounds like fun. Now I can dream about horses and ice cream instead of mean old pirates." She settled her head on the soft pillow and tucked Nelly, her rag doll friend, under her arm. "Good night, Kendall."

"Night, Meg."

28

CHAPTER 4

# MULLER'S

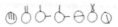

The next day the children went to the beach on Assateague Island, just across the causeway off the coast of Chincoteague Island. They traveled the short distance to the beach in the Walker's van loaded down with towels and chairs, picnic baskets, and beach umbrellas. Assateague Island, a pristine national park, was crowded with families all enjoying the warm sunshine, the rolling waves, and the wide sandy beach.

Once the group had set up their camp for the day, the girls headed straight for the waves. It was fun getting splashed and dunked in the cool, salty water. The boys, however, had a different plan in mind. They walked down the beach a short distance from their group and Brian retrieved a folded paper from his pocket and a map of Chincoteague Island. On the paper he had written the details from Charles Wilson's letter to his brother, details about where the pirate treasure was hidden. The boys studied the map for a long time and were not able to figure out where to start in their hunt for the buried treasure. Wilson's letter was confusing, "...north of the second inlet above Chincoteague Island, Virginia, which is at the southward end of the peninsula."

"I don't know if this means we start above Chincoteague and move further north from that, or start at the south end of the island and then move north," Brian said after pouring over the map for several minutes. "Or maybe it really means that the treasure is on Assateague. This is totally confusing. No wonder no one ever found his treasure." He folded up the paper and the map and stuffed them back in his pocket. "Well, I know who can help us. I know someone who's an expert on Assateague. He knows every inch of this island. He can help point us in the right direction. Then, we'll be on our way to finding that treasure." Brian and Jack walked along the beach, watching children playing in the waves. "We need to start working on the treasure hunt for the girls," Brian said.

"Okay, I get that we're going to write clues for the girls to follow to find something that we hide, but what are they going to find?" Jack asked.

"How about some buried treasure?" suggested Brian.

"Sweet. Got anything in mind?"

"Stick with me, man. I've got a plan."

The extended Walker family, including the girls and Brian, spent several hours on Assateague, playing in the waves and picnicking on the beach. Later that afternoon, after returning to Aunt Pat's and Uncle Rich's house, the girls took a walk to find the ice cream shop where Ashley worked. They had rinsed off all the sand from the beach and were ready for a cool treat. Mrs. Walker gave them directions and they quickly found themselves on Main Street. They passed rows of little shops jammed with people. The road was filled with cars inching along at a slow pace. There were people everywhere, young and old, all dressed for the beach in shorts, sunglasses, and tee shirts. The sounds of laughter filled the air. And everywhere there were pictures of horses on tee shirts, on book jackets in store windows, and on posters. They stopped in front of one window and gazed at the array of toy horses large and small. "I like the little ones the best," Megan said. "And one could fit in my bag. I have to be careful not to have too much stuff to bring back home on the plane, since I already am going to have to put Nelly in there."

"I'm glad you like that old doll so much, Meg. I know you'll take good care of it. If I brought it home, my brothers would destroy it in a day. They'd take it outside and get it dirty or something."

"I guess I could have given her to Mom and Dad to take back home with them last week, but I didn't think of it. Well, I'll just have to pack her very carefully."

The girls continued down Main Street and there were huge banners stretched across the street advertising the Fireman's Carnival and the Pony Swim and Auction.

"Kendall, what's the difference between a horse and a pony? Everything around here says pony instead of horse. Aren't ponies just small horses?"

"I really don't know. I wonder if Ashley knows anything about horses," Kendall said.

The girls continued down the sidewalk past the movie theater, the Island Roxy. The marquee on the theater invited visitors to go to the Fireman's Carnival and announced daily showings of the movie "Misty of Chincoteague."

"Kendall, have you read that book, 'Misty'?"

"No, have you?"

"No, I haven't either, but I was thinking that it'd be

fun to read, especially now that I'm here on Chincoteague. Maybe we could see the movie one night. Want to?" Megan asked.

"Yeah, that would be cool."

A few blocks further past the busy intersection where the causeway and bridge meet the island, at the corner of Main Street and Cropper Street, was their destination: Muller's Old Fashioned Ice Cream Parlour.

It was in a pretty old house, set far back from the street. The girls walked up the front steps, through the screened-in porch filled with dainty pink and white metal chairs, and in the front door of Muller's. They were greeted by a rush of cool air and the sweet smells of waffle cones, chocolate, and fruit syrups. They waited in line to place their order and took in the sights. There was a menu board listing dozens and dozens of ice cream flavors. Everything sounded delicious. As they neared the front of the line, they saw the glass fronted counter revealing a frozen sea of cool delights. Behind the counter, the green milkshake maker twirled three shakes at a time.

"What can I get for you two?" asked the girl behind the counter. "Oh, hi, it's you!" Ashley exclaimed as she recognized Megan and Kendall. They ordered their cones, then carried the towering refreshments into the pink dining room nearest the counter. The girls sat down at one of several small tables that filled the room. At the center of one wall stood an empty fireplace that probably had not held a fire for years. The dining room was filled with other visitors to Chincoteague who were also enjoying a cool cone and a chance to escape the heat of a Virginia summer.

"Mind if I join you?" asked Ashley as she dropped

into one of the empty chairs at their table. "I'm on my break now. Boy, have we ever been busy. And this is nothing compared to what we'll be doing next week. You know, during Pony Penning."

"Yeah, we saw all the posters and everything about Pony Penning. Say, Ashley, do you know much about horses?" Kendall asked.

"If you want to know about horses, you've come to the right place," Ashley said, settling into her chair. "My dad's one of the firemen who ride horseback and round up the ponies on Assateague, and help swim them across the channel. In a few years, I might be able to do that, too."

"Wow, that's cool," Kendall said.

Megan licked an icy drip that was making its way down the side of her waffle cone. "Ashley, we were wondering about something. What's the difference between a horse and a pony?" she asked.

"Well, ponies are a breed of horse, a certain type of horse, like poodles are a breed of dogs. Ponies are smaller than most other breeds of horses. The Chincoteague ponies are short and stocky. They live off the salt grass in the marsh, which stunts their growth. They live wild, so during the winter they might not get too much to eat. And they drink brackish water." Megan and Kendall looked puzzled. "That's a mixture of salty sea water and fresh water. Chincoteague ponies have adapted to drinking this kind of water over the years."

"How did the ponies get on Assateague Island in the first place?" Megan asked.

"No one knows for sure, but there are two theories. One is that they're from a shipwreck off Assateague in 1820. There were about 100 small ponies on the ship, headed for Spain, I think. Or maybe South America. I forget. People think some of the ponies survived the wreck and swam ashore and adapted to living on the island. The other theory is that these ponies today are descendants of livestock that were kept by colonial people a long time ago. There were horses and cattle and sheep and hogs living on these islands, and maybe the ponies are the great, great, great, grandponies of them," Ashley explained.

"What do you think happened?" Kendall asked.

"I really don't know, but however they got here, I'm glad they're here! I have a Chincoteague pony of my own and I love her," she said.

"You have your own pony?" Megan was impressed.

"Yes, and she's just beautiful. Her name's Star and she's all black except for a white star on her forehead and white just above her feet. She was Queen Neptune five years ago."

"What's Queen Neptune?" Megan asked.

"You guys don't know much about the pony swim and the auction, do you?"

"No, we just know it's going on next week and tons of people come here every year to see it. We haven't had time to find out much about it yet," Kendall said.

"Well," Ashley said as she glanced at her watch, "I have time to give you a quick lesson in Pony Penning." The girls leaned in closer so as not to miss a word. "Every year at the end of July, the firemen here on Chincoteague go over to Assateague on horseback and round up all the ponies. They make noises and holler and crack their whips in the air to scare the ponies out of their hiding places, and chase them into a pen, a big fenced place. That's the Penning part of Pony Penning.

That'll happen next Tuesday. Then the next morning, Wednesday, the firemen will drive the herd of ponies into the channel and swim them over here to Chincoteague."

"Can ponies swim?" asked Megan.

"Yes, they can swim. They swim kind of like dogs swim. Everyone who is helping keeps a close eye on all the ponies, especially the babies, to make sure they make it across okay."

"You mean that the baby ponies swim across, too?" Megan was amazed.

"Of course. The babies, the foals, are the ones who are auctioned off the next day, after the swim." Ashley continued. "Foals are baby horses under a year old. Male foals are called colts and female foals are fillies. The very first foal to reach the shore, whether it's a male or female, is crowned either the King or Queen Neptune. That's what Star was. She was the first foal to reach the shore. The swim's really something to see. People start going down to Memorial Park around 4:30 in the morning. You have to get pretty close if you want to be able to see the ponies in the water. The ponies swim across during what's called slack tide. That's a time when the tide isn't going in or out, so the water's very calm. Slack tide only lasts for about 15 minutes, so as soon as the tide's slack, in go the ponies. After all the ponies get across to Chincoteague, they rest for about 45 minutes, and then they do a run down Main Street to the carnival grounds."

"You're kidding. All those wet horses run down Main Street? Don't they run away or go into stores or people's yards?" Kendall was shocked.

Ashley laughed. "Oh, funny things have happened

before, but the firemen are on horseback and they sur-
round the herd and keep them together. Once I saw a
pony break out of formation and run across someone's
lawn. But a fireman went after it and guided it back to
the rest of the herd. The ponies go into a pen at the carnival grounds until the auction the next morning."

Megan asked, "Did you buy Star at the auction?"

"No, the King or Queen Neptune is kept in a special
pen and then there's a raffle for him or her. I saved my
money and bought a bunch of tickets. My parents
bought tickets, too, and put my name on them. I won
her in the raffle!"

"Wow. You're so lucky," Megan said.

"I really am, I know. But having a horse is a lot of
work." Ashley turned and looked toward the ice cream
counter and saw a long line of people waiting. "I'll tell
you more about that later. I have to get back to work
now. I'm glad you guys came by. It's been nice talking
to you. I'll take you to see Star sometime, okay?"

"Wow, that would be great, and thanks for all the information about ponies. I can't wait to see them next
week," Megan said.

"Me, too," Kendall said. "See you later, okay?"

"Sure. Have fun, you all."

The girls walked back to Aunt Pat's house and felt a
new excitement about the upcoming pony events. The
boys were waiting for them when they arrived home.
"How come you didn't bring us cones?" teased Jack.

"Right. In this heat, we'd need a bucket. You know,
we talked to Ashley at the ice cream place. It's so cool
that she has her own pony," Kendall said.

"Totally. Star's awesome. We've ridden her a few

times," Brian said.

"Yeah, she's a cool horse. But Ashley's been training her for years. It's a lot of work to have a horse," Jack said.

"Ashley said the same thing. I think it'd be great to have my own horse," dreamed Megan.

"It might be hard to put a pony in your suitcase, Meg. How about something smaller, like the stuffed pony we saw in that store window?"

Megan laughed but didn't notice the wink that passed between the boys.

"Can I interest anyone in some pizza and roller skating?" asked Mrs. Walker as she joined the children outside.

# CHAPTER 5

# THE DREAM

As the group entered the front door of the yellow and red building, they were met by a medley of sounds from electronic games, children chattering excitedly, and music blaring from a juke box in the game room on the left. Several families were seated in booths and at the raised counter in the snack bar on the right. A buzzer sounded as the cashier nodded at the door and they entered The Dream. Brian stayed in the game room while the others went straight back through a short hall lined floor to ceiling with photographs of skaters. They entered the large, darkened room that was the skating rink. Music was playing, adding to the excitement of the evening. Mrs. Walker took charge of getting shoes sizes for skate rentals while Jack studied the people already gliding around the shiny wooden arena.

"See anybody you know?" asked Kendall.

"Nope, not yet, anyway, but I thought maybe I'd see some kids from school. Everybody likes to hang out here."

Mrs. Walker waved her hands for the children to join her at the skate counter. Megan hurried up beside her and took in the endless shelves of skates in pairs by sizes assembled neatly behind the counter. She grabbed hold of her skates and carried them to the bench where several people were seated, lacing on their skates. A few moments later, Kendall joined her on the bench.

"This is going to be fun, huh?" Kendall said.

"Yeah. This place is cool. It's like a place I go to sometimes back home with my friends."

The girls tucked their shoes under the bench and stepped onto the smooth wooden rink. The music changed tempo and they watched as the skaters swayed to the beat.

"Let's go," Kendall said as she reached for Megan's hand and pulled her into the swirl of skaters. The girls circled the rink laughing. On the next lap, they caught sight of Jack stepping into the arena but quickly passed him by. "Let's see if Jack can catch up to us." Round and round they went, moved along by the crowd of other skaters. Then Megan felt someone tap her on the shoulder.

"Think you're pretty good skaters, huh?" Jack said as he rolled up along side them. "This is kid's stuff. Now, I'll show you how to really skate!" He moved ahead of them and did a fast turn and was skating backwards, still able to face them.

"Watch where you're going, Jack. There's a ton of people here," Kendall warned.

"Relax. I do this all the time. Watch this!"

Jack turned again with a flourish and faced forward, then zigged and zagged between skaters. When he came to an older couple holding hands, he ducked way down low and scooted under their arms. The surprised couple wobbled and nearly lost their balance. The girls could hear Jack laughing as he disappeared from sight.

"He's nuts," Megan said.

"Boys!" her cousin shook her head in agreement.

They all skated for a long time, all except Brian,

orange cast up to his shoulder, who was playing in the
game room. Then Megan coasted off the wooden plat-
form and sat on a bench to rest. Kendall continued
skating and Megan watched her glide along side Mr.
and Mrs. Walker. The music changed again, the lights
dimmed, and a mirrored ball began to spin on the
ceiling. Reflections of lights danced on the walls, on the
skaters, and on the shiny floor. She saw Jack streak by
again, waving. Megan adjusted her skates and surveyed the other skaters. There were loads of people
skating. She saw one little girl skating between her
parents, holding their hands so she wouldn't fall. There
were couples skating together and teenagers laughing
with their friends. As a group of skaters passed by
where she was sitting, something caught Megan's
attention. There was something familiar about the
fleeting gesture she saw. She leaned forward to tried to
watch the skaters as they rounded the curve but she lost
sight of them in the crowd. A few minutes later, the
lights came back up, the mirrored ball stopped turning,
and as they passed by her again, Megan studied them
more carefully. It appeared to be a family, mother,
father, and a girl Megan guessed to be about her own
age. They were all smiling and seemed to be enjoying
the evening but what caught her attention was the
subtle hand movements they made as they looked at
each other. Megan couldn't be sure of what she saw, so
she waited until they circled the rink again and passed
in front of her. Yes, she thought to herself, they're
signing. She saw the girl close both hands and then pop
her thumbs up, and she sped by. "Fast!" Megan said
aloud.

   "Who are you talking to, kiddo?" asked Brian as he
plopped down beside her on the bench.

"Oh, there are some people out there who are sign-ing, you know, Sign Language."

"Cool. I learned some of that a few years ago at school. At least I know the alphabet." He carefully formed the letters a,b,c, and d.

"You really do know the alphabet," Megan said. "I know the alphabet and I learned how to sign some too, because one of my friends has a brother who's deaf." Megan searched the skaters for the family again. "There they are. The girl has on a yellow shirt, see?" she said as she pointed them out for Brian.

"I see them." He paused to watch with interest. "What are they saying?" he asked.

"The girl just asked her parents if they want to eat," she translated.

Brain studied Megan for a moment, surprised. "Megan, you're pretty cool, for a girl, I mean. And this gives me an idea. We need to come up with a secret code for our treasure hunt, right? How about using Sign Language as our code?"

"How can we do that? You can't write it on paper."

"Oh, yeah, you're right. Well, it seemed like a neat idea anyway." Brian continued to watch the crowds of skaters as they sped by. "You know, those people must have read my mind. I'm ready to eat, too. How about you? Ready for some pizza?"

"Sure. Let's get Jack and Kendall and Jack's par-ents."


A short time later the group was assembled in a large booth enjoying their pizza and sodas. Everyone had enjoyed their skating, that is, everyone except Brian. With his large orange cast propped on the table, he told his friends about his success playing video games. "I got up to almost 2500 points in World of Screech and passed level 8 in Space Jungle. I was okay on Flipped Out Rockers, but I think I need a little more practice on that one. It was cool. There was a big line waiting for Space Jungle, so I did some of the others first and waited until the line got shorter."

Megan wasn't paying much attention to Brian's stories. She was searching the people who were leaving the skating area heading through the game room towards the door to leave The Dream. Then she saw them, the family she had seen signing on the rink. She knew it wasn't polite to stare, but she was fascinated watching them communicate with their hands. Then, the girl happened to look her way and saw Megan watching her. Megan smiled and hesitantly signed, "Hi."

The girl looked puzzled and glanced over at her parents who were having a discussion over an unfolded map. The girl looked back at Megan and Megan smiled again. The girl looked unsure, and then signed a short question to Megan. "Do you sign?"

"Yes," Megan signed from the snack bar with a closed fist that nodded up and down. "A little," she added with a shy smile. She was unaware that the conversation at her table had stopped and everyone was watching her and the girl in the yellow shirt.

"My name's M-A-D-D-I-E. I live in Florida," the girl signed.

"I'm M-E-G-A-N." Megan spelled out her name letter by letter as one does in American Sign Language. "I live in California." She used the sign "gold" that her friend taught her is also the sign for California.

"I came to see the ponies swim. You, too?" Maddie asked.

"Yes. I love ponies," Megan answered.

"Me, too." Maddie looked over at her parents, had a short exchange with them that Megan couldn't see, then signed, "Sorry, I must go now. Nice to meet you, M-E-G-A-N."

"Where are you staying?" Megan signed, but it was too late. Maddie had already turned her head and was leaving. She followed her parents out the door, and left The Dream.

"Megan, I had no idea you knew Sign Language," said Mrs. Walker. "Where in the world did you learn that?"

"Oh, from a friend at home," Megan answered, still watching the door, hoping that Maddie would come back in.

"You never told me you could do that, Meg," said Kendall. "That's so cool. Can you teach me?"

"Yeah, and me, too?" Jack asked.

"Hey, guys, I'm in, too," Brian said.

"Do you know that girl from someplace, Megan?" asked Mr. Walker, but Megan was lost in thought and wasn't listening to any of them.

"She saw them skating just before we came in here to eat. She could tell what they were saying to each other. Isn't that the coolest? I know the alphabet, but that's all," Brian said.

Conversation resumed at their table and everyone finished eating their pizza, but Megan was quiet for the rest of the evening. So many thoughts were running through her head. Seeing Maddie reminded her of her friends back home and made her feel homesick. She remembered how upset she had been before about having to spend the whole summer away from her friends, but then she smiled to herself as she recalled the fun and adventures she and Kendall had had. And now her grandparents would be joining them in a few days, so she didn't feel homesick any more. One other thing was bothering her, but she couldn't quite figure out what it was. She felt like she had almost figured out the answer to a question, but couldn't remember what the question was. It was just beyond her reach.

Kendall was thinking about what a great vacation she was having, visiting her grandparents in Virginia and now staying on Chincoteague Island with the Walker family. Mr. and Mrs. Walker and Aunt Pat and Uncle Rich were making the girls feel like part of the family, and Kendall enjoyed that. It was so nice to be treated like a kid for a change. Back home, she had very little time to enjoy just being a kid. She was too busy taking care of her two brothers. It was wonderful getting a break from all the responsibilities of those two boys.

Kendall was surprised to discover that Megan knew Sign Language. Her cousin was still something of a mystery to her. Megan was very quiet and shy, and she didn't talk about home or her friends or school much at all. Kendall knew that Megan had trouble in school. She had heard her mother talking about it, so she didn't mention school at all around Megan. Kendall, on the other hand, was a very good student. Schoolwork just seemed to come easily to her.

Having both boys, Jack and Brian, there with them was working out better than Kendall had thought. Mrs. Walker had confided in Kendall and told her about the surprise for Jack, that Brian would be staying with them, too. Kendall had been concerned that it would be just like home again, and that she would get stuck watching out for the boys, but it seemed that they were very independent and didn't need her help. In fact, it seemed like they didn't even want her around much, especially Brian. Kendall was intrigued by Brian. He seemed smart and she liked that he read those pirate books and came up with the pirate game for them. But it seemed that Brian didn't like her too much. He seemed to like Megan, though. Everyone liked Megan, Kendall thought, but Megan didn't even seem to know it. Kendall felt a bit jealous of Megan, but then, Megan was so sweet, she couldn't help liking her. She hoped that Megan was having as good a time as she was.

"Megan, are you awake?" Kendall asked from her lower bunk. "You've been so quiet tonight, ever since you were talking in Sign Language to that girl. Are you okay?"

"I've just been thinking about a lot of stuff. I guess I'm a little bit homesick."

"Not me. I'm having so much fun here. And next week we get to see the pony swim and go to the auction. And don't forget about our pirate treasure hunt. The boys are cooking up something, but I don't know what yet. And we have to figure out some kind of secret code. Brian was talking about that again tonight at dinner. He said maybe you would have an idea for one. Do you? Did you think of something?"

"Secret code? I don't know. Can't think of anything yet. Maybe tomorrow, okay?" She closed her eyes and yawned. "I'm tired. Too much pirate beach,pony skate, secret dream code..."

"Meg, what are you talking about? Pirate beach? Pony skate? Megan?"

But Megan was already on her way back to The Dream.

# Chapter 6

# Code Brown

ᚤ⊘◔⊖◯Ⓦ⚬◔◔⊚

When Kendall woke the next morning, she saw Megan sitting crossed legged on the floor, her red leather journal open, holding a pen in one hand while staring at her other hand.

"What are you doing?" Kendall asked.

"Oh, you're awake. Kendall, I figured it out. I'm making up our secret code!"

"You are? How are you doing that?"

"Well, last night at The Dream, Brian had the idea that we could use Sign Language for our code. But I told him it wouldn't work because you can't write in Sign Language. You just kind of do it in the air. Then I had these really weird dreams last night, about Grandma and Grandpa riding horses on the beach, but the horses were wearing roller skates, and then there were these pirates eating ice cream. Then I saw a paper and it had funny things written on it, and when I woke up, I figured out a way to make a code using little pictures kind of like hands doing the fingerspelling alphabet."

"Fingerspelling? Is that what you call it?"

"Yes, because you're spelling words with your fingers," Megan explained.

"Meg, that's really clever. Can I see what you've

done?"

"Sure." Megan scooted across the room and handed her cousin the journal. "This one means 'a', and this means 'b'." She demonstrated how to form the letters with her hand and pointed to the corresponding figures she had drawn. "What do you think?" she asked.

"This is cool. But you're going to have to teach the rest of us the alphabet so that we can read the code."

"Well, Brian already knows it, so maybe he can show Jack and I can show you. It's easy. Want me to teach you how to spell your name?"

By the time the girls were eating breakfast, Kendall was able to spell her own name and was able to form all the letters of the alphabet. She forgot a few sometimes, but Megan was a patient teacher and gently prompted her when needed.

"Kendall, what do you want to E-A-T?" Megan asked, slowly forming the letters with her hand.

"Eat? I want to eat T-O-A-S-T, toast." Kendall replied.

"You're doing great. What do you want to D-R-I-N-K?"

"Frimp? What does that mean, frimp?"

"No, silly, not frimp. Watch again: D-R-I-N-K."

"Oh, drink! I always get 'd' and 'f' mixed up." Kendall laughed.

"Don't worry about it. You're catching on really fast and we can practice as much as you want."

"Practice what?" Jack asked as he joined the girls at the breakfast table.

"Megan's teaching me Sign Language," Kendall announced. "Well, she's teaching me the alphabet right now. I'm learning to fingerspell. That's when you spell

words with your fingers, like this." She demonstrated
for Jack that she could spell her name. "Megan figured
out a really cool secret code for us. Wait until you see
it."

"See what?" Brian asked as he entered the kitchen.

"Megan made up a secret code for us," Jack explained.

"Sweet. Can I see it?"

"I haven't quite finished it all yet, but I have it in my
journal. Here, you can see what I've done so far." She
handed her book across the table to Brian. "I got the
idea from you last night when you said maybe we could
use Sign Language for our code. Then I had some crazy
dreams and in my dream I saw this code written down,
and when I woke up, I started working on it."

"Awesome, kiddo. You saw this in your dream?
Amazing." He looked at the symbols Megan had
drawn on the page of her journal. "I see what you're
doing. You're making up little pictures kind of like
hands doing each letter. Cool, very cool." He studied
each of the entries she had done so far. "I like it. Want
me to help you finish it? You're almost done. Then we
can start writing letters in our code. What do you
think?"

"Okay, that sounds fun. I'm trying to make my code
so that if anyone else finds it, they won't be able to figure it out very easily, like that guy you told us about,
that man who made the number code that no one has
ever been able to crack."

"Oh, you mean Beale. I think your code's really
good. No one will be able to figure this out!"

"And I thought maybe you could teach Jack the fingerspelling alphabet. He'll need to know it to figure out
the code. Kendall's getting the hang of it already. Then

we'll all know it."

"Totally. Then we'll have our own secret code, just like the pirates did," Brian said.

"Pirates? Are you kids still talking about pirates?" asked Mrs. Walker as she joined the children at the breakfast table.

"Mom, those pirates were cool. Real tough dudes," Jack said.

"Then we'll certainly want to be sure to get you kids over to see the exhibit of the treasure coins. I'd like to see them myself. I've never seen anything like that before. There was an interesting article about them in the newspaper, and Aunt Pat has seen the exhibit and said it is great. Would you like to go?" she asked.

"Yes, ma'am, that would be cool," Brian said. "We'd all like to go, right?" He looked at his friends who all happily nodded in agreement.

"Wonderful." She turned to Jack. "I'll check with your dad and see when he thinks would be a good time to go. We don't want to go when there will be a long line, and I imagine loads of people will be going to see this exhibit."

"Cool, Mom."

She turned to Megan and Kendall. "Your grandparents will be here tomorrow. Do you think they'd like to go, too?" she asked.

"I'm sure they would. They love old stuff, like antiques and things. I think they'd like it," Kendall answered.

"Then that settles it. We'll go tomorrow, after your grandparents get here. It's just a few blocks away, over at the Chamber of Commerce building," said Mrs. Walker as she washed dishes in the sink.

"Megan, let's get that code finished, okay?" Brian

said, chewing on a piece of toast.

"Fine with me." They left the table and the screen door smacked closed behind them leaving Kendall and Jack behind.

"Pretty cool code Megan thought up, huh?" Jack said.

"Yeah, she's quiet, then she just comes up with these clever ideas."

"Brian always has neat ideas, too. He reads a lot and gets ideas from stuff he reads."

"I like to read a lot, too, but I don't get ideas from what I read. I just read, you know?" Kendall said.

"Hey, I don't even like to read, so don't look at me. So, Brian's a cool guy, don't you think?"

"He's okay. I don't think he likes me much, though."

"Oh, don't worry about that. He's doesn't like girls," Jack explained.

"He seems to like Megan," Kendall said.

Jack just shrugged his shoulders.

After lunch, the boys went off on their bikes announcing that they would check out the carnival grounds, but after a quick stop at the carnival, they hurried to see Brian's Assateague Island expert. Before the boys left, Aunt Pat reminded Brian that he had to be very careful on a bicycle with his broken arm, and he promised to be. The code was finished and written in Megan's red journal. Brian named it "Code Brown" since Megan's last name was Brown.

The girls took a leisurely stroll downtown. They stopped into a busy store and purchased pony postcards to send to friends and family. They also bought pocket-sized notebooks and pens for writing their secret messages. They mingled with the rest of the tourists along Main Street and then headed up the front walk of their new favorite spot, Muller's Old Fashioned Ice Cream Parlour, to cool off.

Ashley was behind the counter again and helped the girls select from the long list of inviting flavors. They settled themselves behind their tall cones at a small table next to the fireplace in the pink dining room. For a few moments they took in the sweet smells of chocolate and waffle cones and cooled off in the air conditioning, then they flipped open their new notebooks and got down to work.

"I need to make a copy of the code for each one of us so that we can all have it. Then we can write messages for Brian and Jack and see if they can figure it out." Megan opened her backpack and pulled out her red leather journal and copied the coded alphabet onto a piece of notepaper for Kendall. While Kendall studied the code, Megan made two more sets of Code Brown and tucked them into the back of her journal for safe-keeping. "Now, let's practice writing something in code. What about our names?" Megan referred to her coded alphabet and carefully penned:

"That's cool, Meg. I'll try writing my name." She looked at the alphabet Megan had written down for her as a guide. Slowly, Kendall drew out the symbols in Code Brown for her name.

"What do you think?" she asked her cousin, show-ing Megan what she had written in her notebook.

Megan studied Kendall's encoded message:

"That's great. I want this to be really hard for anyone else to figure out. Maybe we shouldn't leave a space between words. Instead, since most of the letters have a circle with some lines, let's use just a plain circle where we want a space. That'll really make it tricky. What do you think?" she asked.

"Good idea. In case someone finds one of our messages, we don't want them to be able to figure it out." She filled in the space between her first and last names with a circle. "Yeah, that makes it really tricky, you're right, Meg. The boys are going to love this!" She continued to practice drawing the coded symbols. "We can write a message for the boys and give it to them at dinner tonight," Kendall said while she wrote her name again.

Megan had been looking up from their table studying the fireplace beside them. The house was very old and the years were evident in the beautifully worn wood floors and aged bricks. As her eyes traveled up to the old wooden mantle, what caught her attention was a narrow painted door on the side of the chimney. "Kendall, what do think that's for?" asked Megan, pointing out the wooden hatch.

"It reminds me of some of the doors we found in Grandpa's cottage when we were looking for Anah's secret door. It's cool, don't you think?"

"Yes, and it gives me an idea." Megan lowered her voice and glanced at the tables around them to make sure none of the other guests were looking their way. "Can you open it? Let's see what's inside," she whispered.

"Megan, I'm surprised at you. You're getting brave!" Kendall smiled fondly at her cousin, then stood up and carefully opened the little door a few inches. Inside were shelves holding an uninteresting array of glasses and other small items, probably put there many years ago and forgotten. She closed the door and sat back down. "So, what's your idea?"

"We could put the boys' messages in there. And they could put ours in there, too. It can be our secret place for exchanging messages. First, we can write them a message, in code of course, and tell them to find the next one inside that cupboard. After they get it, they can leave one for us. What do you think?" she asked.

"That's so cool. I love it! You know, I don't think your mother is the only one in your family with ideas about mysteries. Megan, you have some good ideas. You should write these ideas down in your journal and show your mom. Or maybe just write down things we do, like a diary. Later, you might want to write your own story or something. What do you think about that?"

Megan considered what Kendall had suggested. "I'm not sure. I don't write very well. I always have trouble in school with writing, and my teachers know my mom and think I should be able to write great stories. But I can't." She thought some more. "But I guess it might be fun to just write down things we do this summer, so that I can remember everything later." Megan looked directly at her cousin. "Kendall, thanks for being so nice to me. Before I came here this summer, I had heard a lot about you from my mom. 'Kendall is so smart.' 'Kendall is so responsible.' 'Did you know Kendall can cook? Kendall got another award in school.' I wasn't too happy when you showed up at the airport, but now I'm really glad you're here. You're really smart and everything else my mom said, but you're also really nice. You treat me like just another kid, not like a little kid. It seems everyone else treats me like a little kid. I know I'm not very tall, but I'm almost the same age as you and Jack and Brian." Megan looked down at the table. "Anyway, I just wanted to tell you that."

Kendall smiled at her cousin. "Thanks, Meg. I'm glad you're here, too, and I can't wait for Grandma and Grandpa to get here tomorrow. I miss them." She looked down at their papers with their names written in code. "So, now we need to write some messages for the boys. One that tells them to come here and look inside the cupboard, and another one that's going into the cupboard. What's that one going to say?"

"I don't know. Maybe it can just say something about ice cream or, I can't think of anything right now. You think about that one, okay? I'm going to write one that tells them to find their message here." Megan hunched over her journal and began to carefully encode the first message for Brian and Jack.

"Let's see," said Kendall. "We could say something about the pirate treasure we're going to see tomorrow. Yeah, that'll be good." She began writing her message to the boys.

When the girls were finished, they checked both messages for accuracy. When they were satisfied that everything was correct, Kendall carefully folded her message. She opened the chimney cupboard door again and quickly tucked the paper inside. Megan's message to the boys was put into the back of her journal along with the two sets of Code Brown.

The girls were very excited as they headed back to Aunt Pat's house. They knew the boys would enjoy the secret message hidden at Muller's and they were looking forward to seeing their grandparents the next day. As they walked along, Megan continued helping Kendall with fingerspelling. She would slowly spell out a word with her right hand and Kendall would guess the word. Kendall was catching on very quickly and the game was fun for both girls.

A block before they arrived back at Aunt Pat's and Uncle Rich's yellow house, Jack and Brian called out their names. The girls turned as the boys rode up beside them.

"We found some pirates, you guys!" Jack said, hopping off his bike.

"Pirates? What are you talking about?" asked Kendall.

"Well, they're not really pirates, but we saw these two strange dudes over by the marina. They're probably fishermen, but they were acting kind of weird. I named them Blackbeard and Billy Blads. The Blackbeard guy is kind of greasy looking and has a beard and a pony tail and Billy Blads is a shorter guy with short wavy hair that looks like it's painted on his head," Brian said.

"Brian, what's that other name for pirates you told us about?" Jack asked.

"You mean 'freebooters'?"

"Yeah, freebooters. I like that. We saw a couple of 'booters' this afternoon," Jack said.

"Where did you get the name Billy Blads?" asked Megan.

"There was a pirate from Rhode Island who was

named William Blads. I like the name. Blads sounds like bads, and he must have been a bad guy, because he was executed for being a pirate," Brian explained.

"You sure know a lot about pirates," Megan said.

"Well, I've been reading those books. It's pretty cool stuff." Brian carefully got off his bike and walked with the girls to Aunt Pat's house.

"What have you two been up to this afternoon?" Kendall asked.

The boys looked at each other and smiled. "Just riding around and checking on the carnival and stuff. There sure are a lot of people in town now. I guess they're starting to arrive for Pony Penning next week," Jack said. "What have you guys been doing?"

Kendall looked at Megan as if to ask permission, and Megan nodded. "We've been practicing with the code. In fact, we have something for you," Kendall said.

With that, Megan opened her backpack and retrieved her leather journal. She opened the back cover, pulled out several small sheets of paper, and handed them to Brian. "Here are your copies of the code, and a message. See if you can read it," she said. "Oh, and I put in a circle instead of leaving a space between words, just to make it harder for anyone else to figure out in case they find it," she added.

Brian unfolded the sheets and saw Megan's symbols covering the pages. "Come on, Jack, we've got work to do," Brian said. They boys hurriedly parked their bikes on the front lawn and dashed to the house.

"Wait 'til you see the surprise we have for you," Jack called out over his shoulder as he raced through the front door.

## CHAPTER 7

# MISTY

"Megan, honey, phone call for you," Aunt Pat called. "It's your mother."

Megan scrambled up the front steps and into the house. While she was inside talking to her mother, Ashley drove up in her pick up truck.

"Hey, Kendall. I forgot to ask you and Megan if you want to go with me later to see 'Misty'. It's playing at the Island Roxy. Want to go?" She climbed out of the truck and walked closer to where Kendall was standing.

"Oh, yeah, that would be neat. I'll go ask if we can go. Megan and I were talking about that earlier today. Neither of us have read the book and we thought it would be nice to see the movie, especially with Pony Penning next week."

"We should go early, because there will be a long line to get in. There always is," Ashley explained.

"So, you've seen the movie before?" Kendall asked.

"Oh, I see it every year. I love it! You guys have to see it while you're here. It's great. It's an old movie, but it's really nice. If you want to go, just come on over and get me. We should leave here about 4:00."

"Okay. I'll talk to Megan and ask Mrs. Walker and make sure it's okay for us to go. I'll let you know if we can go."

"Great. See you later," Ashley said as she entered

her house.

Kendall went into Aunt Pat's house to find Megan. "How's your mom?" she asked when she met Megan in the kitchen.

"She's fine, and so's Dad. I told Mom all about our secret code and the pirate coins we're going to see tomorrow and the beach and skating and everything we've been doing. She's already started working on our book! She said it's coming along great. And I told her Grandma and Grandpa are coming tomorrow and that we're going to Pony Penning next week. And I told her that you suggested I use my red journal like a diary and that I've started writing down things we've been doing this summer. She was really happy about that."

"That's good. Ashley came over and invited us to go with her to see 'Misty' at the movies this afternoon. Do you want to go?" Kendall asked.

"Yes, I'd love to go. But we need to ask Mrs. Walker if it's okay first."

"Ask me if what's okay?" asked Mrs. Walker as she entered the room.

"Ashley asked us to go with her to see 'Misty' at the Island Roxy. Do you think that would be okay?" Kendall asked.

"Of course. You girls will love it. I've seen that movie more times than I can count. What time do you want to leave?"

"Ashley said we should leave about 4:00 because there will be a long line," Kendall answered.

"A long line where?" Jack asked as he and Brian came into the kitchen.

"A long line at the movies to see 'Misty'. Do you guys want to come with us?" Kendall said. "We're going with Ashley."

"I've seen that movie a ton of times," Jack said. "What do you think, Brian?"

"Oh, let's go. I've seen it too, but it'll be cool. All the kids in town will be there, you'll see. Every family that comes for Pony Penning goes to see 'Misty' at least once while they're here. It's part of the experience!"

"Great! I'll go tell Ashley that we're all going with her. She said we should leave early because of the long line to get in," Kendall said as she hurried out the door to find Ashley.

After an early dinner, the kids were all on their way to the movies. The girls were walking ahead with Ashley, asking lots of questions about Star. The boys were a few paces behind. A dirty black pick up truck passed them slowly. Brian happened to glance at the license plate that read BTB 1724. "Hey, those are my initials, BTB, and 1724, that's the year my pirate book was published. Look, Jack, isn't that cool?"

Jack looked to where Brian was pointing and saw two scruffy men in the truck. "Aren't those the pirates," he said.

"Pirates?" Ashley said, turning. "What are you talking about?"

Brian confirmed that the two men in the truck were their pirates. "Yeah, that's Blackbeard driving and the other one is Billy Blads, his partner in crime."

The girls didn't get a good look at the men in the truck before it passed them by. "Too bad we missed them. I want to see what those guys look like," Kendall said.

"Not me. I don't want to see any pirates, real or pretend," Megan said.

"Come on, Megan, it's just for fun," Brian said.

"They aren't real pirates, but it's fun to pretend they are, don't you think?"

"They're freebooters. Booters ahead in a black pick up truck, guys," Jack said to his friends, laughing.

"Okay, who's going to tell me what's going on with these pirates," Ashley said.

Brain explained about the two men that he and Jack had seen and that they had given them pirate names just for fun. "They're probably fishermen, or are here for Pony Penning or something, but we decided to pretend they're pirates." Then Brian filled Ashley in on some of the information he'd been reading in his pirate books.

"That's pretty cool stuff, Brian. Do you guys know about the treasure coins they have over at the Chamber of Commerce building?"

"Yeah, we're going to see them tomorrow, after Grandma and Grandpa get here," Kendall said. "Want to come with us?"

"I can't. I have to work tomorrow. But tell me about them, okay? I'll try to get over there one day to check them out," Ashley said as they arrived at the theater. They lined up behind several families waiting for the ticket window to open. Within a few minutes, the line extended half way down the block.

"You were right about lots of people coming here. Look at the line!" Megan said.

Jack was looking over the crowd for familiar faces, and Brian was doing the same.

"Hey, there they are again," Brian whispered, elbowing Jack in the ribs with his big cast as he pointed to two men walking on the other side of the street.

The girls looked, too, and saw the men Brian was pointing to. The taller man had greasy-looking long hair pulled back in a pony tail and a dark, scruffy beard. The man next to him also had dark hair, but his was oddly short and wavy, and did look like it was painted on his head, just as Brian had described him.

"Are those the pirates?" Kendall whispered.

"Yeah. Maybe they're coming to see 'Misty'," joked Jack.

"You sure found yourself some good pirates, Brian. Those guys are strange looking. I've never seen them around here before. And they don't look like fishermen, either. What's with the tall guy having one pant leg rolled up?" Ashley asked.

"Beats me. Maybe he's making some kind of pirate fashion statement," Jack said, laughing.

"Maybe he rides a bike. I know some guys do that so their pants don't get stuck in the chain," Kendall suggested.

Megan frowned as she looked across the street at the pirates. "They look creepy to me. The shorter guy has no neck and beady eyes. Maybe they really are pirates."

"Megan, remember, we're just pretending they're pirates. They're probably tourists here for Pony Penning, just like us." Kendall looked down the block at the long line of people patiently waiting to see 'Misty'. "Hey, isn't that the girl you were talking to at the roller skating rink?"

"Where? Do you see Maddie?" Megan followed Kendall's gaze and indeed she saw Maddie waiting near the end of the line, along with her parents. Megan waved, but Maddie didn't see her. "I'll run down and say, 'hi'. I'll be right back," Megan said to her friends. But just then, the ticket window opened and the line moved quickly into the building.

"There's no time now, Meg. Maybe you can find her

after the movie."

Disappointed, Megan followed her cousins and Ashley and Brian into the theater.

Two hours later, the crowd poured back onto Main Street as the movie theater emptied for the night. "That was great, wasn't it?" Ashley said. "How did you like it?"

"It was sad, but I'm glad they let the Phantom go back to Assateague. She wasn't happy being in a pen, even though she liked running with the kids. I was glad she got to go back to be with the Pied Piper," said Kendall.

Megan looked around at the people coming out of the theater, searching the crowd for Maddie. Sadly, she didn't see Maddie or her parents. "Do you think Misty stayed with Paul and Maureen? I wasn't sure at the end of the movie," Megan said.

"Yes, I think so. Weren't those foals cute? That's what Star looked like when I got her. She was just a few months old," said Ashley.

"Ashley, I was surprised how little the ponies were in the movie. I know that the babies, I mean the foals, are the ones that get sold, but they're really small, like big dogs. And the full grown ones still seemed pretty small, like maybe too small for adults to ride. Is Star small like that?" Megan asked.

"No, Star's pretty big. But that's because she doesn't eat the salt marsh grass anymore. You'll have to see her sometime. All the ponies that live on the mainland grow a lot bigger than the ones who live their whole lives out on Assateague. I think that the Chincoteague ponies are bigger now than they used to be, too. Other types of horses are getting mixed into the herd now, so the ponies are larger than you saw in the movie."

"And Misty was so cute! I would love to see a pony like her," Megan said. "Maybe we'll see one like her at the pony auction next week."

"Hey, Megan, you know who you remind me of?" Brian asked.

"Who?"

"If you put your hair in braids, we could call you Maureen. And Jack here looks a little like Paul. If anyone decides to remake 'Misty', you two could be the actors!" Brian said.

Jack laughed. "And your grandparents could be Mr. and Mrs. Beebe."

"Grandma and Grandpa are nicer than those guys were." Megan walked along the sidewalk watching the crowd disperse. "I'm glad Grandma and Grandpa will be here tomorrow. I can't wait to tell them about seeing 'Misty'.

"What did you think of the pony roundup in the movie? My dad will be doing that next week. And in a few years, I hope I get to join them," said Ashley.

"I didn't know there were so many ponies on Assateague. It was so cool seeing them all running. They're so pretty. And I was worried when little Misty was swimming across and Paul had to jump in and help her. I hope nothing like that happens this year," said Kendall.

"Don't worry about that. The firemen and the other volunteers really look out for the ponies. There are lots of people in the water watching them, more than you see in the movie. It's very safe for the ponies. And they keep the foals with their mothers until they're old enough to be on their own." Ashley turned to face the girls. "Did I tell you about the 'give back' ponies?"

"No, what are those?" Kendall asked.

"Oh, I've heard of those," Jack said. "That's when people buy the ponies at the auction but give them back to the fire department, right?"

"Yes, and they give them back so the pony can live free all its life, just like the Phantom did. If that pony gets rounded up the next year and swims over here for the auction, it isn't sold. The firemen go through the herd and separate out the ones who are the 'give backs' and make sure they aren't sold to any one ever again," Ashley explained.

"I like that idea. I think it would be nice to have a 'give back' pony. Can you go to Assateague and ride it sometimes?" Megan asked.

"Yo, Megan Maureen, didn't you see the movie?" asked Brian, laughing. "Those ponies are wild. You can't just walk up to a wild pony and hop up on its back and take a gallop down the beach. They have to be tamed, you know, gentled, like the kids in the movie did. And that takes a long time. Isn't that right, Ashley?"

Megan felt embarrassed.

"Brian's right. It took me a few years before I was able to ride Star. I had to get her used to me and then used to having something light on her back for a long, long time before I could think about riding her. In the movie, when the kids got the Phantom, she wasn't a foal. I think they said she was a three year old pony. So she was just about old enough to ride, but she had to be trained, or gentled, first. But with Star, I had to wait until she was full grown and strong enough first, and used to me. If you try to ride them too young, they can get spooked and it can also hurt them. Training a horse is a lot of work. But for me, with Star, it was worth it."

Ashley pointed down the street to a pretty house. "That's Miss Molly's over there," she said. "The lady who wrote the book, 'Misty of Chincoteague', Marguerite Henry, stayed in that house while she was writing the book. Pretty cool, huh?"

"Really, that's her house?" Kendall asked.

"No, it's not her house. It's a bed and breakfast, like a guest house, and people stay there and eat some of their meals there. But Marguerite Henry was staying there while she was writing 'Misty'.

"She's right. I've heard that, too," Brian said. "She's a famous author. She wrote a bunch of books, all about Misty and other ponies." Brian turned to face Megan. "Your mother's an author, right?"

"Yes," Megan said quietly, still feeling uncomfortable.

"So, is she famous? Like, do people know who she is when you go places and stuff?"

"I don't know. I guess she's a little bit famous. She's in magazines sometimes and she's been on TV before," Megan explained.

"Really? That's so cool. I didn't know she was famous," Jack said. "I knew she was a writer, but I never thought much else about it. Like, if we went to a bookstore, would we find books there that she wrote?"

"I guess so."

"Megan, what's your mother's name?" Brian asked.

"Rachel, Rachel Brown."

"Your mom's Rachel Brown?" Ashley asked, stopping abruptly. "I didn't know that. I know who Rachel Brown is. She writes mysteries, right?"

"Yeah, and she's writing a book right now about us, me and Megan and Jack, and the stuff we found, the letters and the diary, and the book and the other stuff.

Right, Meg?" Kendall said.

"Well, when I talked to her tonight before dinner she said she's already working on it."

"Maybe we'll be famous," Kendall said as they arrived at their houses. "Or maybe your mom will come here to write the book and stay at Miss Molly's, too."

"Get a grip, Kendall. We're in the story, but we aren't writing it. I don't think you need to start planning what to wear for your first TV appearance," Jack teased.

Ashley waved good night to the kids as she headed to her front door. "Good night you guys. It was fun. Come by Muller's tomorrow if you get a chance, okay?"

"Thanks for inviting us to see 'Misty'. It was great. We'll see you tomorrow," the girls said.

"Bye, Ashley. See you later," the boys said.

"Girls, I suggest you bone up on your secret code because tomorrow you're going to have some messages to read," Brian said as they entered Aunt Pat's house.

"Well, you guys better practice, too. Did you figure out your message yet?" Kendall asked.

"No, we didn't have a chance to do it before dinner, but we're going to work on it now. Just remember, there might not be any real pirates here, but there might be some real treasure on Chincoteague Island," Brian said.

"Treasure? What kind of treasure?" Megan asked. But the boys just laughed and ran ahead of them up the stairs.

## CHAPTER 8

# KNIGHT RIDER

ᚥ⚭ᚤ☌☌⚭⚭ᚥᚥᚥᚥᚥ

The next morning, the Kellam's kitchen was bustling with activity. Aunt Pat and Uncle Rich left just as the girls were getting up. "See you kids over at the Chamber later. I'm working there today. I volunteer in the office during the summer, especially around Pony Penning time. I know you're going to enjoy seeing the treasure coins. They're really interesting," Aunt Pat said as she collected her things and headed out the door with Uncle Rich. He was going fishing with a few of his friends.

"Catch some big ones for dinner, Rich," Mr. Walker called out as he entered the kitchen. "Your grandparents should be here soon," he said to the girls, who were busy pouring bowls of cereal. "I talked to them last night while you kids were at the movies and they're anxious to see the coin exhibit with us today."

"Where are the boys?" Kendall asked.

"Oh, they're probably upstairs. They had breakfast a little while ago and I think they went back upstairs. They're up to something. Don't know what," Mrs. Walker said as she scrambled some eggs for her husband. "I'm glad you enjoyed the movie last night. Perfect timing on seeing it, what with Pony Penning and the auction next week."

"Have you girls ever been to an auction," Mr.
Walker asked. Then he stopped himself with a laugh.
"Oh, yes, you certainly have. How could I forget? But
this auction will be very different than the auction you
went to with your grandfather last month. All that will
be for sale this time is ponies, lots of ponies."

The boys were on their bikes headed for Muller's
Old Fashioned Ice Cream Parlour. "I wonder what time
this place opens up," Brian said.
"Oh, it should be open by now. Ashley has to go in
to work early to get things ready for the day. And in
this heat, people want ice cream almost 24 hours a day,
at least I do!" Jack said.
"I'm not exactly sure what the girls' message
means." Brian stopped in front of Muller's and got off
his bike. He pulled the folded paper from his pocket
and read what he and Jack had written below each of
Megan's coded symbols.

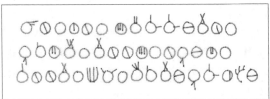

GO TO MULLERS PINK ROOM OPEN
DOOR BY FIREPLACE.
"Well, there must be a fireplace in there somewhere.
I've never noticed it before, but how hard can it be to
find it? Then, we'll look for a door. Maybe it goes
down to the basement or something," Jack said. "This
reminds me of us looking for the secret door last month
in Anah's cottage behind their grandparents' house."

"That must have been awesome, dude," Brian said as the boys sprinted up the front steps of Muller's.

"Yeah, it was pretty cool."

They entered the building and immediately bumped into Ashley, who was carrying a tall stack of paper ice cream cups.

"Hey, guys, a little early for ice cream, don't you think? Were you looking for me?" she asked.

"Oh, no, we were thinking about getting some ice cream later and wanted to see what flavors you have to-day," Brian lied. "Don't worry about us, we know our way around."

"Okay, fine with me. We're not really open yet, just getting stuff ready."

"Don't let us bother you," Brian said as Ashley headed past them into the back to stock the shelves.

"That was some quick thinking, my man," Jack said to his friend.

"Yeah, thanks. Now let's find us a pink room with a fireplace, okay?"

They quickly found the dining room to the left of the front door that was definitely pink in its decor. And the old fireplace stood just as it had for over 100 years. But there didn't appear to be a door anyplace.

"Now, what could the girls mean? There isn't a door here," Jack said to his friend.

"Maybe we got the message wrong." Brian pulled it back out of his pocket and smoothed the paper on the top of a small table near the fireplace. The boys sat down and looked at the message carefully, comparing the symbols with their copies of the code that Megan had drawn for them. "We got it right the first time. It definitely says, 'open door by fireplace'," Brian said,

shaking his head in confusion. He looked up at the fireplace and noticed, for the first time, the small cupboard
door on the left side of the chimney wall. "Hey, I never
saw that before, did you?" he whispered.

Jack jumped up and moved quickly to the door.
"I've been here about a million times and never saw it
either. It's just like in the old cottage." Jack looked
around to make sure Ashley and the other workers
were busy and not watching them and slowly opened
the door. Brian was right behind him, pressed up close
to the side of the fireplace. There inside the door, on a
small shelf, was a folded up note. They quickly retrieved it and Brian stuffed it in his pocket and headed
out the front door calling to Ashley as they left, "Bye,
Ashley, see you later!"

Outside, the boys sat right down on the steps of
Muller's and pulled out their copy of Code Brown to
decode the message they had just found in the secret
fireplace cupboard.

"That was a totally awesome hiding place for this
message, don't you think? We should leave our messages for the girls here, and use this place as our meet-
ing place, too. Especially since the girls will probably
be staying with their grandparents at the campground
now. This code stuff is sweet!"

"Yeah, really cool. Let's see that message," Jack said.

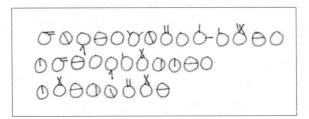

The boys sat quietly with pens and paper pulled from their pockets, deciphering the message letter by letter. "It says, 'Hope you like the pirate treasure.' "Hey, dude, this code stuff is fun. They must be talking about the pirate treasure coins we're going to see today. Now, we have to write a message back to the girls. We need to write two, actually, one to give them that will let them know to come here, and a second one that can be their first clue to find their hidden treasure. That one we'll have to hide back in the fireplace cupboard. Let's start with the first one." After a moment or two of thought, Brian burst into a wide smile. "I have an idea!" he said as the two boys started writing their messages, letter by letter, in their secret code.

A car pulled up in front of the neat yellow house on Chincoteague Island. "Grandma!" Megan called out as she raced outside to greet her grandparents. Kendall joined her and the foursome walked together with arms linked into Aunt Pat's and Uncle Rich's house. Mr. and Mrs. Walker were there and told the Bayleys what pleasant house guests their granddaughters had been.

"I'm not the least bit surprised. These girls are delightful. I'm so glad they were both able to come for the summer," Grandma said.

"So, when do we get to see those treasure coins? I read about the exhibit in the newspaper and have been wanting to get up here and take a look," Grandpa said to Mr. Walker. "I think there will be someone over there today to answer questions and tell us more about the coins. Today is the perfect day to go see them."

"We were just waiting for you all to get here." He turned to his wife. "Are the boys still upstairs? I haven't seen them for a while. They're awfully quiet."

Mrs. Walker called up the stairway, "Jack, Brian, come on down. Mr. and Mrs. Bayley are here. We're ready to go." There was no response from the boys.

"I'll go get them. They're probably reading more of Brian's pirate books," Kendall said as she headed up the stairs.

"Pirates? What's this about pirates?" Grandpa asked Megan.

"Brian, Jack's best friend, brought a bunch of books about pirates and he's been telling us about them."

"You know, Megan, there were pirates out on Assateague Island several hundred years ago. I imagine there are some buried pirate treasures here someplace, unless they were already dug up. Interesting folks, those pirates," Grandpa said. "As a matter of fact, a friend of mine at the newspaper said that there are relatives of Blackbeard still living here in on the Shore."

"Really? Still? You should talk to Brian. He knows a lot about pirates." She was interrupted as Kendall bounded back down the stairs.

"They aren't up there. I looked out the window and their bikes are gone." She turned to Mrs. Walker. "Where do you think they went?"

"I have no idea. Those boys." She shook her head. "I'd hate to go without them, but there's no telling where they are or when they'll be back."

"Why don't we go to the campground and get settled in and have some lunch. By the time we get back, I'm sure the boys will be here. Then we can all go together. How's that sound?" Grandpa asked Mr. and Mrs. Walker.

"That'll be fine. Sorry about this, Warren. But you

know these boys!"

"I'd rather get moved in first anyway," Grandma said. "Are you girls coming to stay with us?" she asked.

"Yeah, and we're already packed," Kendall said.

Grandpa slowly guided his car next to a large metallic blue recreational vehicle and came to a stop. "This is it," he said.

"Wow. It's huge. We get to stay in this?" Kendall asked, pointing to the RV.

Grandma laughed. "Yes, at least for the next week or so. Our friends keep it here for most of the summer and then travel around with it in the winter. It was very nice of them to let us use it, don't you think?"

"I'll say. I've never been inside one of these. Have you, Meg?" Kendall asked.

"No, but I've always wanted to see what they look like."

"Let's get our bags out of the car and into our new 'cottage'!" Grandpa said.

The RV was very roomy inside. In the front were two big, comfortable seats for the driver and a passenger when it was on the road. Behind that was a living room with a television and a dining area which connected to the kitchen. There was a small bathroom with a shower and a little tub, a small bedroom with bunkbeds, and a larger bedroom in the rear for Grandma and Grandpa. The girls were amazed at how compact everything was. There were drawers and storage closets in every imaginable place. The kitchen was complete with all necessary appliances, but all were just smaller versions of those you would find in a house.

"This place is so cool. It's like a big dollhouse,"

Megan said, delighted with their room.

"Yeah, you could really live in here, couldn't you Grandma?" Kendall asked.

"Lots of people do, especially after they retire." She finished putting away clothes into drawers. "For me, I prefer a house and a garden, but for a vacation, it couldn't be better."

"Come on out and see what I have here," called Grandpa from outside.

The girls climbed down the steps and watched as Grandpa pulled a barbecue from a big storage compartment on the side of the RV. Then he reached back inside, picked up something large, and set a blue two-wheeled bicycle on the ground. "This one's for you, Kendall. I thought you'd like blue the best." He reached back in and pulled out a second bicycle, this one yellow. "Megan, this is for you. Isn't yellow one of your favorite colors?" he asked.

"Oh, yes, Grandpa. It's beautiful," Megan said as she touched the black leather seat and the white basket attached to the handlebars.

"Grandpa, do these belong to the people who own the RV?" Kendall asked.

"No, they belong to my two granddaughters," he said with a smile. "I bought them at an auction last weekend and brought them up here yesterday. I came up with my friend so he could show me how to work this thing," he said, pointing to the RV. "And I brought up a load of groceries so we'd be all set to go when we got here."

"Thank you, Grandpa, so much. I love my bike," Megan said.

"Me, too. Mine's so pretty." The girls gave their

grandfather a hug.

"I thought you could use them when you're here this summer, and then we'll put them away until next year. We're hoping you girls will come every summer for a visit."

Grandma came out of the RV and admired the bicycles and the smiles on the girls' faces. "Your grandpa always finds great things at his auctions, doesn't he?" she said.

While they were eating lunch in their miniature kitchen, Grandpa told the girls about the newspaper article he had read that discussed the treasure coin exhibit they would be seeing that afternoon.

"There will be a large number of silver cobs in the exhibit," he began.

"What's a cob?" Megan asked.

"It's a handmade coin. A certain weight of silver was cut off of a bar and then rather crudely stamped with its value. They were stamped a little like when you stamp sealing wax on a letter or envelope. Do you know what I mean?" he asked.

"Yes, I've seen that on the backs of special letters or invitations my parents have gotten," Megan said.

"How old are the coins in the exhibit?" Kendall asked.

"Says in the paper that they are mostly 17th and 18th century, so that's coins from the 1600s and 1700s. Pretty old, I'd say."

"Wow, that's even older than the stuff we found at the auction, right?" Kendall said.

"Yes, even older than the book you kids found. Now, besides the silver cobs, there are a number of very valuable gold coins in the exhibit, too. I'm anxious to

get a look at them. I read something else interesting
that I didn't know before. Back in colonial times, the
shopkeepers really had to know their coins. You know,
the coins that people used for trade, to buy things,
weren't American coins. We didn't start making our
own U.S. Minted coins until the late 1790s, and then
only an a pretty limited basis."

"So what kind of money did people use?" Kendall
asked.

"Mostly Spanish coins, and then coins from other
countries that immigrants brought with them, as well,
but I imagine we'll see a lot of Spanish coins in the exhibit."

"Weren't there a lot of coins from England in colonial America?" Kendall asked, remembering the history
lessons she had read in school.

"Actually, England didn't want their coins used in
America for trade, so most of the English coins went
back to England as taxes. I suppose people and busi-
nesses paid their taxes to England using English coins.
So, no, there weren't too many English coins in circula-
tion." He looked at the article which he had carefully
saved from the newspaper. "There's a list here that tells
what the denominations are of these early coins." He
showed the list to the girls.

"So, a 2 real coin was also called 2 bits, and that was
like our 25 cents. And a 4 real was 4 bits and that's 50
cents," Kendall said.

"Two bits, four bits, six bits, a dollar. All for the
cougars, stand up and holler!" Megan said with a wide
smile.

"Hey, I heard that cheer before, too. I never knew
what two bits and four bits were. Neat!"

"These were the Spanish denominations, the reales, and when the U.S. began minting coins, we used the same denominations: 25 cents, 50 cents, and a dollar."

Grandma began clearing the table and the girls got up to help her. "One other thing you girls might find interesting about these old coins is that sometimes people cut up the coins. For example, if a man had an eight bit coin and owed someone four bits and he didn't have a four bit coin, he would just cut up his coin and give the other man the part he owed. You might hear the expression sometime, 'pieces of eight'. That's what it refers to, pieces of an eight bit coin. It would be like if you had a one dollar bill and owed someone 50 cents, and you just tore the bill in half. But we can't do that now. Back then they could do it with the silver and gold coins because the values were based on the weights of the precious metals they used."

"Grandma, how did you know that?" Megan asked.

"Your grandmother was a teacher and she's read hundreds of books," Grandpa said, winking at Grandma. "Well, we best be off now so we can see those coins. I'm anxious to see a real gold doubloon. And there's a special coin there called the Knight Rider. I want to see that. This afternoon, the man who owns the coins will be there to answer questions. I certainly hope they have good security at the exhibit. These coins are quite rare and very valuable," Grandpa said.

## CHAPTER 9

# TREASURE COINS

○○○○○○○○○○○○○○○

The girls and their grand-parents went back to the Kellam's house and met Mr. and Mrs. Walker already in their van and ready to go. The group traveled the short distance to the Chamber of Commerce building in two vehicles. The boys, who had returned home while the girls were at the campground, rode in the Walker's van. They all parked in front of the Chamber building, a long, grayish-blue modern wooden structure. The parking lot was full but there was no line outside.

The party entered the building and immediately saw the treasure coin exhibit to the left. There were several dozen people crowded around it, reading the descriptive cards that gave a detailed account of the items on display. More people were standing and listening to a man dressed in a suit and tie. He stood out from the crowd of tourists in their shorts and tee shirts. Soon they made their way to the front of the group and saw what everyone had been looking at. Inside a large glass box was a pile of silver coins, about as many as one could hold in two hands. Then there were individual coins, each with a small card next to it, explaining the coin's origin. Some of those were gold and some were silver.

"Wow," Brian whispered. "Real pirate treasure."

"Awesome. Look at these things. They must be really old," Jack said.

The girls were right behind the boys. "Where were you guys earlier, when my grandparents got here? We were all looking for you," Kendall asked.

"Out," Jack said, not taking his eyes off the coins.

"Yeah, I guessed that." She looked into the glass display box. "Are these actually pirate coins?" Kendall asked.

Brian was busy reading the informational cards around the exhibit. "It says here 'these irregularly shaped coins are called cobs. The term cob comes from Spanish cabo de barra, meaning cut from a bar.' See, some of these things aren't round like coins today. They look handmade, don't you think?"

"Yeah, they're made like you stamp sealing wax," Kendall said. "They cut off some of the silver and then stamped it to show the denomination. Did you know that sometimes people even cut up the coins to make change?"

"Where did you hear that?" Brian asked.

"From Grandma."

He continued reading. " 'A bar of silver was sliced into smaller pieces, heated, and quickly stamped with the Spanish royal arms.' I guess these are all Spanish coins," he said.

"Yes, because in colonial America they used mostly Spanish coins. The English people didn't want the Americans to use their coins so they made them pay their taxes to England using English coins," Kendall explained. Brian grumbled and continued reading to himself.

Grandpa came up behind the children. "These Spanish coins are made from gold and silver that was mined in Mexico and Peru. The Spanish people set up mints near their mines and made these Spanish coins from the gold and silver ore. They're very old, from the early 1600s to the mid 1700s. See, this one is from 1638 and this one was made in 1724."

"1724? That's the year my pirate book was first written. How cool is that?" Brian said.

"It says that the big silver ones are called pieces of eight. Pieces of eight what?" Jack asked.

"Eight reales, or eight bits," Kendall answered.

"It's a measurement of coin value," Grandpa explained to the boys. "Then the smaller ones are four reales, two reales, one real, and the smallest one is a half real. It says that 16 of these large silver pieces of eight are equivalent to one of these gold doubloons." He indicated the big gold coins shining under the display lights.

"That's 128 bits," Kendall said. The rest of the party turned to face her. "Grandpa said 16 of the eight bits equal one gold doubloon. 16 times eight equals 128," she said, smiling.

"What are you, some kind of math whiz?" Brian asked.

"No, well, I am pretty good at math."

The man in the suit walked over to where they were standing, admiring the coins. "Can I answer any questions?" he asked. "I'm Daniel Ashford from Treasures of Maryland."

"Are these your coins?" Brian asked.

"Yes, they are. I'm a coin collector and a coin dealer.

I'm also a relic hunter of sorts," he added.

"Relic hunter? What does that mean?" Jack asked.

"I like to hunt for these old coins. And along the way, I often find other old relics, Indian arrow heads, old buttons, pieces of pottery, articles like that," Mr. Ashford said.

"So you found all these coins?" Brian asked, amazed.

"No, only some of them. Here, let me show you some of these coins." He walked to the display case, with Grandpa and Grandma, Mr. and Mrs. Walker, and the children all listening with great fascination.

"I heard you talking about the cobs," he said, pointing to the large pile of crudely formed coins. "A couple hundred years ago, Spain had colonies in South America. A lot of silver was being discovered and the King demanded that it be sent to Spain as quickly as possible. Rather than taking the time to make evenly milled coins, coins that would look a lot like our coins today, a faster method was used. A bar of silver was cut into small chunks of precise weights. These chunks were then hammered with dies that imprinted information on them, like the denomination, the assayer's initial, where it was made, and some designs indicating it was a Spanish coin, such as the shield you can see on some of them."

"The assayer is the person who weighs the coins, right?" Mr. Walker asked.

"Yes, that's correct. And even though some of these coins are over 250 years old, you can still make out some of that information." He pointed to a cob at the edge of the pile. "For example, on this coin, we can make out quite a bit of information, even though it is rather irregular and crudely made." Everyone leaned forward to get a closer look at the coin he was pointing to. "This is a very typical cob. It's a two real coin. You can see the number 2 right there. And the face value is like our quarter. It was made in 1741, and you can clearly see the 41 right there, just above the wave design. The letter P indicates that it was made at the Potosi mint in Bolivia. You can see an assayer's mark as well." The group was silent, studying the coin Mr. Ashford was describing.

"If you'd like, I'll tell you about the four featured coins in this exhibit. These are special coins that each have their own story to tell. The first one is this large silver dollar. It's often referred to as the Knight Rider, and if you look closely at the picture on the coin, you'll be able to see why." There, pictured clearly on the front of the grand old coin, was an armored knight on horseback. "This is a Dutch Colonial Lion Daalder, a silver dollar, and it was made in 1711 in Holland. It was found on the shipwreck of a ship called The Love. The Love was on its was from Amsterdam to the East Indies when it went down. It was over 150 feet long and carried about 40 guns."

"Love Boat and the Knight Rider. I like the sound of that. So cool," Jack said. Mr. Ashford smiled. He was pleased that the children and their family were so interested in the coins.

"How did The Love go down? Did pirates sink it?" Brian asked.

"Interested in pirates, are you? So am I, but I don't think pirates had much to do with this ship sinking. It was probably just a bad storm. But pirates were very active at the time and did steal a huge amount of coins much like these."

Mr. Ashford pointed to the next coin in the row. "This next coin is a four escudo gold doubloon. The date on this coin is 1791, and it was made in Madrid, Spain. The four escudo gold coin had a face value of eight dollars, but it's worth much more than that to-day."

"How much is it worth?" Brian asked.

"I'd say this coin is worth at least $500."

"Wow, then all these coins together must be worth a fortune," Jack said.

Mr. Ashford continued. "The doubloon is the most legendary colonial coin of all time. Many pirates and colonials lost their lives in the quest to acquire these romantic coins. The importance of Spanish money in the American colonies can't be overstated. It's been estimated that over half of the coins in colonial America were Spanish and also legal tender here until 1857." Mr. Ashford paused, then pointed to the shiny gold coin. "What you might want to know about this particular gold doubloon is that it was found in a field, a farm field, not far from here."

"Really? Just laying on the ground? Where?" Brian asked with growing excitement.

"I found it myself a few years ago. It wasn't laying on the ground, but it wasn't too deep, either. I use a special metal detector when I'm relic hunting. It's quite an exciting hobby, a real adventure. I search in fields, with the owner's permission, of course, and look for signs of a house that may have been there over 200 years ago."

"How do you know where to look?" Kendall asked.

"There are certain indicators I look for. Sometimes I

find pieces of broken pottery, pieces of old brick, and
those help me pinpoint where a house used to stand.
The houses have been gone for maybe a hundred years,
and now the land is farmed. I wait until the fall, after
the harvest is the best time. Then, the ground is cleared
of plants and the soil is freshly turned, and treasures are
often waiting, hidden just beyond sight."

"Is this the only coin you've found in a field?"
Grandpa asked.

"Oh, no, I've found hundreds of coins this way. Of
course, I don't find them all at once. But sometimes, I
do find many all in a pretty small area. You see, a long
time ago, people stored their money in jars or pottery
vessels and buried them in the ground for safe keeping.
Sometimes, the owner of the jar of coins died, and no
one knew where it was buried. Years later, when a
farmer was plowing that land, his plow might have dug
down and hit the jar and broken it, spreading the coins
with the plow. I've found many coins that are pretty
close together, and pieces of jars and pottery, too."

"This is so cool. So, do you have any coins that came
from pirates?" Brian asked.

"The third coin washed up on the beach here on Assateague," Mr. Ashford said.

"You're kidding. Really?" Jack said. "And you
think pirates had something to do with it?" Jack looked
at Brian.

"I believe so. It's an eight real coin, a silver dollar,
made in 1738 in Mexico. It has reeded edges, see the
pattern around the edge, like on our quarters and fifty
cent pieces. Most of our coins today don't have smooth
edges. There's a good reason for this fancy edge, and
it's not to make the coin look pretty. Some people used

to tamper with their coins, clip or cut the edge off of them, to get more silver. With these irregular cobs, or these other coins without a design on the edge, no one but an assayer would know that some of the silver had been removed. Then, the person would save all the filings and eventually melt them down and have a new coin."

"Awesome. Did pirates do that?" Brian asked.

"It does sound like something pirates would do, and maybe some did. But mostly, the pirates just stole the coins and anything else they could get their hands on. I believe this coin is part of some pirate's booty and eventually washed ashore."

"So, there really were pirates around here?" Megan asked.

"Absolutely. Lots and lots of them, in fact. Assateague was one of their hideouts for years. It's not uncommon for old coins like these to wash ashore from time to time. Who knows? There are probably other stashes of pirate coins someplace around here, too."

The boys looked at each other again. This was just the information Brian needed to confirm the importance of his pirate treasure quest.

"The fourth coin is a 1776 Spanish silver dollar, eight reales, made in Mexico. You can see a circle over the letter M, and that indicates Mexico. An M with a crown over the top means it was made in Madrid. This coin is very special because of the year, 1776, the year of our independence from England. Coins made in that year are extremely collectable and you just don't see them often."

"You sure know a lot about these coins," Kendall said, impressed.

"I enjoy them, and enjoy learning about them. And the best part is hunting for them, whether in a field, or at a coin auction. It's all an adventure, as far as I'm concerned." More people had joined their group, listening intently as Daniel Ashford spoke about his coins. "Can I answer any other questions?" he asked.

"Why do so many of the silver cobs have holes in them?" Mrs. Walker asked. "Were they used as jewelry?"

"That's a very good question. Many people think that, but actually, people strung these types of coins onto a piece of leather and tied it around their wrist for safe keeping." He pointed to one very small cob at the edge of the pile. "Do you see that small heart-shaped cob? The heart-shaped coins were made for Spanish royalty. So, they're rather special coins." Mr. Ashford smiled at the children, then moved over to another group of interested tourists who had more coin questions for him.

The girls leaned close to the display and looked at the little heart-shaped coin. "How neat, don't you think?" Megan said to Kendall.

"Yeah, so cool. I never knew any of this stuff."

"Me, neither."

The children spent more time looking at the coins and then the boys went to the information counter to see if they could find out more information about the coins. They were surprised to see Aunt Pat behind the counter.

"How do you like those coins? Pretty neat, huh?" she said.

"Totally. Do you have any other information about them, like a brochure or something?" Jack asked his aunt.

"Yes, we do. I'll get one for you." She moved away from the counter and the children looked around at all the people in the room getting information about hotels, restaurants, and most of all, Pony Penning.

"Jack, look over there," Brian whispered and nodded his head in the direction of the coin exhibit. Jack turned his head and saw exactly what Brian had seen. Leaned over the glass display box were two men, dressed much like the rest of the tourists in the room. But it was obvious to both boys that those men were their pirates. They were standing close together, probably reading the information cards.

At the same time, Megan and Kendall were standing with their grandparents, looking at colorful brochures about Chincoteague. Megan looked over at the coin exhibit and saw the two men. She tapped Kendall on the arm and fingerspelled one word: P-I-R-A-T-E-S. Kendall strained to figure out the word and Megan repeated it. She knew that Kendall understood her when a surprised look came to Kendall's face.

"Really?" she whispered.

"I think so. Let's ask the boys."

They joined the boys at the counter where Aunt Pat had just handed them a slim brochure about the treasure coin exhibit. Megan caught Brian's eye, nodded toward the exhibit, and fingerspelled the word to him: P-I-R-A-T-E-S.

"Yeah, that's them," he said softly. "We just saw them, too. Wonder what they're doing here?" They watched as the pirates left the coin exhibit and walked over to the information counter a few feet from them. A woman waited on them and gave them a map.

"We should get going," Grandpa said and he and Grandma came over to the girls. They waved good-bye to Aunt Pat and headed out the door.

As everyone got ready to leave, Brian handed a folded paper to Megan. "Here, take a look at this," he said.

Megan glanced down at the paper and could see that it was covered with her secret code symbols. She smiled and put it into her pocket.

Kendall and Jack were talking next to the Walker's van. "I wonder why the pirates were here," Kendall said.

"Pirates? What are you talking about?" Mr. Walker asked.

"Oh, the kids are playing pirates these days," Mrs. Walker explained to the adults who all chuckled.

"Well, I'd play pirates if I was your age, too. Maybe you can find a buried treasure while you're at it," Grandpa said, and the boys looked at each other and smiled.

# CHAPTER 10

# MADDIE

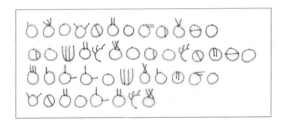

The girls were seated at a picnic table outside the RV, busily decoding the secret message Brian had slipped to them when they were leaving the treasure coin exhibit. They wrote a letter underneath each coded symbol to uncover the communication from the boys.

IF YOU HAVE A BUCK
A CONE WILL BRING YOU LUCK

"Hey, it rhymes! 'If you have a buck a cone will bring you luck.' I know they're talking about ice cream cones, right?" Kendall said.

"Yes, they probably want us to go to Muller's. I don't think they're going to meet us there, because they don't know when we'd be going. I bet they put another message inside the secret door, just like we did. What do you think?" Megan asked her cousin.

"Yeah, I'm sure they did. I'll go ask Grandma if we can ride over to Muller's. It can't be too far from here,

can it? We can try out our new bikes!" Kendall
bounded up the few steps and entered the RV to speak
to Grandma.

Just then, Megan noticed a girl walking a short distance away, at another campsite. She was certain it was
Maddie. The girl happened to turn her head to look
around and saw Megan. Both girls exchanged smiles.
Megan waved her hand for Maddie to come over to the
picnic table. Maddie walked over and said, "Hi, M-E-
G-A-N. You staying here?" She made a sweeping mo-
tion with her hand to indicate the campground.

"Yes, I'm staying there," and she pointed directly at
the metallic blue RV nearby.

"Pretty. Your family's?"

"No. I'm staying with Grandma and Grandpa. This
RV is their friend's. Where are you staying?" Megan
asked in Sign Language.

"There," Maddie answered, pointing out a mid-
sized camper trailer not far away with a striped awning
overhanging a picnic table. "I'm here with my mother
and father," she explained with her hands.

"Nice," Megan said, sliding her right palm across
her left palm. "I saw you last night at the movies. Did
you like it?"

"Yes, I love M-I-S-T-Y. I read the book at school."
Maddie glanced down at the table and saw the coded
message from the boys and Megan's copy of Code
Brown inside her opened leather journal. "What's
that?" she asked with interest.

Megan wasn't sure what her new friend would think
of their code. She hoped Maddie wouldn't think it was
silly.

"Wow. Who made this C-O-D-E ?" Maddie asked,

looking carefully at the symbols Megan had made from the fingerspelling alphabet.

"Me," Megan said, pointing her index finger at herself.

"Why Brown?" Maddie asked, looking at the title Megan had penned at the top of her coded alphabet.

"My last name is Brown," Megan said, moving the inside edge of her flattened left hand down her cheek, making the sign for the color brown.

"Oh, she's here," Kendall interrupted, as she hopped down the steps and came back to the picnic table.

Maddie looked at Kendall and then at Megan with a puzzled expression that Megan understood meant, "Who is that?"

"This is my cousin, K-E-N-D-A-L-L," Megan signed, tapping her cupped left hand along her jaw to indicate a female cousin.

"Nice to meet you," Maddie signed.

Kendall turned to Megan. "What did she say?"

Megan smiled, knowing that Maddie could understand Kendall by reading her lips. "She said it's nice to meet you."

Maddie looked down at her watch. "Sorry, I have to go. I'm going shopping with my parents. Maybe I'll see you later?"

"Yes." Megan smiled and nodded her head.

"I want to see your C-O-D-E again, okay? Great idea, your C-O-D-E Brown."

"Thanks," Megan signed, moving her fingertips away from her lips, almost as if she was blowing a kiss.

With that, Maddie turned and hurried off to her campsite where Megan saw her parents waiting. Then the three of them walked out of sight, but Maddie

turned at the last minute and waved to Megan and
signed, "Later."

Kendall and Megan easily found their way to
Muller's and parked their new bikes in front. Megan
pulled her backpack from her bike basket and the girls
mounted the steps, anxious to find their next message.
They waited in a long line, enjoying the cool air and the
delicious aromas. Finally, it was their turn to order.
    "Hey, guys, how are you doing? Are Jack and Brian
with you?" Ashley asked.
    "No, I don't know where they are. We're not staying
at Aunt Pat's anymore. We're staying at the campground with our grandparents," Kendall explained.
    "Oh, well, they came here early this morning, before
we opened, in fact, and said they'd be back later."
Megan and Kendall looked at each other and smiled
knowingly. At least they knew where the boys had
been part for of the morning. Ashley picked up a scoop
and a waffle cone and asked, "What can I get for you today?"
    The girls found a table in the pink dining room but a
couple was occupying the table nearest the fireplace.
As the girls enjoyed their cool treats, they plotted their
move to the fireplace cupboard.
    "As soon as those people leave, let's just move to
their table," Kendall said, looking for a simple solution
to their problem.
    "But what if they take a long time? What if we finish
eating and they're still here?" Megan was anxious to re-
trieve their message and see what the boys had written.
"Maybe we can distract them somehow and one of us
can slip over and get the message."

"Megan, you're sounding like some kind of a spy!"

Just then, the couple left the table by the fireplace and the girls hopped up and sat back down at the vacant table. After checking to make sure no one was watching, Megan reached over, opened the cupboard door just a few inches, and saw what she was looking for. She closed the door and quickly unfolded the paper she had in her hand. She eyed the carefully drawn symbols, and pulled her journal and a pen from her backpack. Together, she and Kendall deciphered the message that read:

THERES A BURIED TREASURE WAITING FOR YOU CAN YOU FIND IT WAIT FOR A CLUE.

"Hey, another rhyming message! This is fun. Wait for a clue? Is there another paper inside the cupboard?" Kendall asked.

Megan checked, but she had retrieved the only paper inside. All that was left were some old bottles and other uninteresting objects. "No, that's it. Maybe we have to check back tomorrow or something." She thought for a moment. "I wonder what they've hidden for us?"

"I don't know, but we need to hide something for them, don't you think?"

"Yeah, but what? I don't have anything good we can hide. Do you think Grandma does?"

"Not here, not in the RV. If we were at their house, we could go with Grandpa to an auction and get something funny."

"Yeah, that would be good. But we need to find something pretty fast and then figure out where to hide it. The boys are ahead of us in this buried treasure game," Megan said.

The girls left Muller's and headed back to the campground, but decided to go a different way than they had come, to better learn their way around the island. They came upon several families having a large yard sale together. With so many people in town for the upcoming Pony Penning activities, there was a large crowd of people examining the rows of tables covered with items for sale. The girls parked their bikes and joined the shoppers.

"Maybe we can find something for the boys," Kendall said as she looked over a table covered with an odd assortment of tools. "Hey, here's something that you need, Megan," she said as she looked down at several small suitcases and tote bags. "You're going to need something to take stuff back home in."

The girls knelt down on the lawn and carefully looked over each bag. They dismissed most as either too small or too worn. But there were two nearly identical tan bags that seemed nice. Megan thought that Nelly, her rag doll, along with her new journal and anything else she collected while on vacation, would fit easily in the tan bag. Kendall opened each one and discovered that the inside of one was torn slightly, so she zipped that back up and handed Megan the better bag. "Do you like it?" Kendall asked.

"Yes, it's nice. But how much does it cost? I don't have very much money," Megan said.

"I'll go ask. Why don't you look around and see if you can find something for the boys. And I'll look over there," she said, pointing to tables on the other side of the lawn.

Megan walked along slowly, surprised at how many things were there for sale. She picked up a package of markers which were marked "25 cents" and decided to test them to make sure they weren't dried out. She uncapped a black marker, made a few lines on the side of a cardboard box, and turned to find Kendall. As she turned, a man moving quickly bumped right into her, nearly knocking her over. Her hand with the black marker made a long line down the side of the bag he was carrying. It looked just like the tan bag Kendall was carrying for her.

"Stupid kid. Watch where you're going, idiot," the man muttered under his breath, and continued walking rapidly toward the street.

Megan was so startled, she just stood there, feeling embarrassed. Her eyes followed the back of the man and it appeared that he hadn't noticed the mark she had made on his bag. She started to take a deep breathe to relax, then nearly choked. The man turned and headed up the sidewalk away from the yard sale and she got a look at his face. It was Blackbeard! She recognized the long hair pulled back in a pony tail and the bushy, black beard. She stood still for a moment, trying to compose herself. Then she saw that she still had the marker in her hand, but had lost the top. She bent down to look for the cap and saw a piece of paper with a colorful photograph of a pony on it. She picked up the paper, found the top, recapped the marker, and put it back on the table. She looked again at the paper and saw that it was a flyer advertising the movie, "Misty". There were some lines drawn on the back, but it didn't effect the photo and Megan thought it would be nice to take this home to show to her parents and her friends. She folded up the paper and reached into her backpack, found her journal, and tucked it safely inside the red cover.

Megan moved on to the next table, resuming her search for something for the boys. There were books of all sizes and shapes. Most of them were standing up on edge so that the titles were visible on the spines. She scanned what seemed like hundreds of books and then came to a stop. She read aloud, "A General History of Pirates," and laughed. Perfect, she thought and smiled.

"Hey, Meg, I found something," Kendall said as she joined Megan at the book table. Kendall was holding several small toy figures of pirates. "What do you think of these?" she asked.

"They're great. Look what I found," she said and held up the pirate book. "We can hide all this stuff for the boys, don't you think?"

"Sure. These toys are only fifty cents for all of them and how much is the book?"

"The sign says 'Books $1.00'. I think this is like one of the library books Brian has. Did you find out how much the bag is?" Megan asked.

"Not yet. I got busy looking at all the toys. I'll go ask that lady over there. She seems to be in charge."

Kendall was gone just a few minutes and Megan continued looking at the interesting items for sale.

"You want to hear something funny?" Kendall said when she returned. "The lady said that she was glad I'm buying this bag. Oh, it's only two dollars, which is great, don't you think? She said that there were two of them, but someone just walked off with the other one and didn't pay for it. Can you imagine?"

"Oh, really?" Megan said slowly, then decided not to tell Kendall about seeing the pirate. Besides, what did it really matter that she'd seen him? She was still feeling rather unsettled about the incident, especially with the man calling her stupid and an idiot, and she didn't want to think about it again. She was pretty sure it hadn't been her fault, but that pirate gave her the creeps. She wished that the boys had never seen those men.

The girls paid for their purchases and Megan hid the pirate figures and the book in her backpack, just in case they ran into Brian and Jack on their way back to the campground. Kendall slung the long strap of Megan's tan bag over her shoulder and the girls rode their bikes down the streets of Chincoteague, pleased with their treasures to hide for the boys.

# CHAPTER 11

# CLUES

ॐ ᚠ-ᚦᚢ☉

That same afternoon, Jack and Brian were busy making up clues and writing them in code for the girls. Jack was still having a difficult time remembering the fingerspelling alphabet that Brian had shown him, so he had to depend on his copy of Code Brown to draw the secret messages letter by letter. Since Brian was already familiar with fingerspelling, he was able to work much more quickly on his stack of clues.

They had a pretty good idea about where they would hide each clue, but needed to double check on a few places, just to be sure. This treasure hunt was fun, and they knew the girls would enjoy following the trail that would lead them to their surprise. It wasn't exactly a pile of pirate treasure coins, but it was something they were certain the girls would like.

While Brian was writing the coded messages, he thought about the Charles Wilson treasure again and felt certain that he and Jack would be able to find it. After listening to Daniel Ashford at the coin exhibit, he was even more sure of his plan. Besides, his Assateague Island expert had given them some very helpful information that should get them at least pointed in the right direction. One thing was troubling him, though. Jack had wanted to let the girls in on their secret, but Brian had been adamant about keeping the girls out of it. But as Brian was getting to know the girls better, especially Megan, he was beginning to see that perhaps Jack had been right. The code that Megan had made up showed Brian that she was very clever, and perhaps that kind of thinking could come in handy. But Kendall was another matter. Brian wasn't quite sure how he felt about her. She could be bossy at times, and that might present a problem. Brian liked to be in charge and didn't plan on stepping aside to let some girl tell him how to run his treasure hunt. At least this treasure hunt they were on with the girls, secret code and all, would keep the girls busy and distracted and they wouldn't notice when the boys had to slip out to search for the Wilson treasure. Brian found the letter from Charles Wilson and he planned on being the one to find the elusive treasure. But it was going to be difficult and maybe they needed all the help they could get. After all, hundreds of people before them had tried, unsuccessfully, to find the treasure. On the other hand, the girls would soon be gone back to their families far away and he and Jack could be there to get all the glory of being treasure seekers. Yes, he concluded, it was best to keep the Wilson treasure a secret just between Jack and him. Who knows, he thought, maybe they would find their own Knight Rider and some gold doubloons.

Brian gathered up all the clues they had written so far and put them in his pocket. Jack picked up the rest of the papers and pens and their copies of Code Brown and carried them upstairs to their room while Brian told Mrs. Walker that they were going for a walk downtown.

The boys headed straight for Main Street, the center of commercial activity on Chincoteague Island. They needed a few things and knew they would be able to find them in the hardware store. They were so busy talking about their clues and making up more rhyming messages that they didn't notice the other customers entering Showard Brothers Hardware ahead of them. Brian started looking for two of the items on their list, masking tape and string, while Jack just wandered around the store, enjoying looking at the diverse assortment of fishing and crabbing supplies. He was thinking about getting a new crap net so that he and Brian could go crabbing, and this was definitely the place to find it.

Jack couldn't find masking tape, so he went up to the counter and waited his turn to ask the clerk where he could find it. There were several customers ahead of him. His mind was still on clues for the girls when he overheard the clerk say to the men in front of him, "A crowbar? We probably have one, but I'll have to check in the back. Anything else I can help you gentlemen find?"

"Yeah, we need a lot of stuff," the taller man said, reading from a small scrap of paper. "You got any glass cutters?"

"And wire cutters, we need a heavy pair of wire cutters, and some gloves, too, two pairs," added the shorter man.

Brian stood as if in a trance as he recognized the strange, wavy hair of the one man, Billy Blads, and the greasy pony tail of his accomplice, Blackbeard, dressed in a dirty white tank-style undershirt.

"Hey, Bri, I--" Jack stopped talking as soon as he saw the pirates standing there in front of Brian.

"What else do you have on your list, there. Let's see, a shovel, a hammer, nails, plywood. We don't have whole sheets of plywood right now."

"No, we don't need a whole sheet, just a small piece to, oh, to ..." stammered Billy Blads.

"To cover up a broken window until we have a chance to replace it," Blackbeard finished, flashing Blads a stern look. "Oh, and we can't forget duct tape," he said.

"Do you need window glass?" asked the clerk.

"What would we need window glass for?" asked Billy Blads.

Brian and Jack saw Blackbeard elbow Blads in the side. "Not right now. We'll get the glass later." He looked at Billy Blads. "But there are a few more things we're going to need. Maybe we'll look around while you're getting the stuff in the back," Blackbeard said.

As the pirates turned, Jack and Brian ducked behind a stack of crab traps, hoping they wouldn't be noticed. The pirates went down an aisle and the boys could hear them talking.

"Check this out. Perfect. Closed." Both men laughed.

Brian and Jack looked at each other, puzzled. They weren't able to see what the men were talking about.

A short time later, the clerk returned and Blackbeard went back to the counter. "So what brings you gentlemen here to Chincoteague? Here for the pony auction?" asked the clerk.

"No, fishing," Blackbeard said.

The clerk started to bag the items and Billy Blads joined them at the counter with several smaller items and one large item that the boys couldn't see clearly. "So, how's the fishing going?" the clerk asked Billy Blads.

"How the heck would I know?" Blads answered, scowling.

The clerk looked confused, but quickly finished up and the two pirates walked past where the boys were hiding and they heard Blackbeard say to Billy Blads, "Idiot. Keep your mouth shut next time." The pirates walked out of Showard's carrying several large bags.

The boys forgot all about why they had come to the hardware store in the first place and started walking down Main Street, looking through the crowds of people, hoping to spot the pirates or their black truck.

"What do you think those guys are up to?" Brian asked his friend as a funny feeling started gnawing at his stomach. "I don't like the look of those guys. And I think they're not just here to fish or go to the pony auction. There's something creepy about those guys."

"I don't know. They're probably fishermen or some kind of repair men. We really know how to pick our freebooters, huh, Bri? Of course, if they are fishermen, they didn't even have fishing boots on. What kind of booters are they, without even having boots? I guess you could say they are free of boots, so they're freebooters, huh, man?" Jack joked.

"Shut up, Jack. What are you babbling about, anyway? We need to keep an eye out for these guys. I have a strange feeling about them. I kind of wish we'd never seen them in the first place." He looked down the street, past scores of tourists crowding the sidewalk. "You don't think they could really be pirates, do you?"

"Pirates, real pirates? You mean with the guns and the ship and the black flag and everything?" Jack looked at his friend and laughed. "Are you nuts? Get a grip, man. This pirate stuff is starting to effect your mind."

"Well, maybe not pirates, but, you know, maybe something like pirates. I don't know what they're doing, but I have a real bad feeling in my stomach every time I see them."

"Then why are we looking for them? Let's just go home and forget about those two creeps. Besides, we have plenty to think about. Hey, we forgot to get the stuff we need at the store. Did you forget we have one treasure to hide and another to find?" Jack said.

They returned home, with Brian wishing he could tell the girls about their sighting of the pirates. He thought a few more pairs of eyes around town couldn't hurt. He wouldn't tell them much, but just ask them to be on the alert in case they spotted the guys. Brian wanted to know what the pirates were up to. The bad feeling in his stomach was growing. But there was no way to get over to the campground that evening. Aunt Pat had invited Brian's mother over for dinner and the boys had to be there.

The boys were restless during dinner. Brian's mother was concerned about his arm and wasn't very happy that he had been riding a bicycle with his cast. She reminded him, again, that if he fell, he could have a much more serious injury. Mrs. Walker overheard the boys talking about the pirates. "They're still playing their pirate game, I see," she explained to Mrs. Belote. "Well, it's nice. I'm glad that's keeping them busy."

Then Brian had an idea. After dinner was finished, he excused himself from the table and motioned to Jack to join him upstairs. "Let's see if Ashley will drive over to the campground and give the girls their next clue. And we can write another note and tell them to keep

their eyes peeled for the pirates. I don't like those guys.
I think they're up to something."

"Oh, Brian, they're probably here doing work on
someone's house or something, don't you think?"

"I don't know, man, they were acting strange at
Showard's. I'd feel better if the girls were looking
around for them, too. Maybe we can keep an eye on
them and see what they're really doing here. If we see
them working someplace, fine, that's cool. But I have a
bad feeling about them."

Ashley was happy to take the notes to the girls. "I
haven't seen where they're staying yet, but I did see
them today at Muller's. Yeah, I'll stop by and give them
the notes. This is part of your pirate game, right?" Ashley asked.

"Yeah, kind of. Thanks, Ashley. We owe you one,"
Brian said as she left.

Ashley pulled her truck up near the Bayley's campsite. She saw Megan and Kendall and another girl sitting at the picnic table. Grandpa was nearby, cooking
on the grill.

"Hey, Ashley," Kendall said.

"I'm here on a mission," she said, smiling. She
handed two folded pieces of paper to Kendall. "These
are from Brian and Jack. I'm their delivery person
tonight," she said. She looked at Maddie and said, "Hi,
I'm Ashley."

Maddie smiled and looked at Megan. Megan
pointed to Ashley, then looked back at Maddie and
spelled A-S-H-L-E-Y.

"Nice to meet you," Maddie signed.

"She said it's nice to meet you," Kendall explained,

beaming as she recognized what Maddie signed. "She's deaf, and Megan knows how to talk in Sign Language to her. Pretty cool, huh?"

Ashley didn't know what to say, so she pointed to the notes and said, "Aren't you going to read them?"

Kendall unfolded the papers and saw that one was written in code and one was not. She handed the coded message to Megan and read the other aloud, "Keep an eye open for pirates."

Maddie read the paper Kendall had in her hand and asked Megan, "P-I-R-A-T-E-S? What's that mean?"

"Oh, we're just playing a game with my cousin, J-A-C-K," she signed, tapping her cupped left hand up near her hairline to indicate a male cousin. "We saw some strange men and P-R-E-T-E-N-D they are P-I-R-A-T-E-S." She fingerspelled the words when she didn't know the signs.

Maddie nodded. "Fun."

Megan turned her attention to the other note, the one in code. Ashley and Maddie were curious about it and Megan explained to both that this was part of their pirate game. Megan got out her journal and opened it to the page labeled "Code Brown" and began to decipher the message, writing letters under each symbol. Since she had made up the code, she was able to do it quickly.

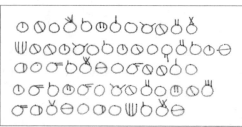

TO FIND YOUR BOOTY ITS QUITE A HIKE
GOOD THING YOU NOW HAVE A BIKE.

While Ashley, Kendall, and Megan talked about what the message meant, Maddie was studying Code Brown.

"I like this. Can you draw one for me, please?" she asked Megan.

"Sure," Megan answered. She started to write down the symbols but Maddie stopped her.

"Later, tomorrow. Not now. Your friends are here. Your code is C-O-O-L."

Megan was pleased that her new friend liked her fingerspelling code.

"Time to eat, girls. Ashley, would you like to join us? Megan, ask Maddie if she would like to eat with us," Grandpa said.

Ashley had to leave and Maddie had eaten earlier with her parents and needed to go back to her campsite. The girls joined their grandparents in a delicious meal and told them about seeing the "Misty" movie the night before and showed them the treasures they had found for the boys at the yard sale. Grandpa was enthusiastic about the treasure hunt. "Now, you need to write clues for the boys. Think of the clues like puzzle pieces. When they have all the pieces, they'll be able to solve the puzzle."

# CHAPTER 12

# JOLLY ROGER

∿⊘ঠ-ঠ-ⴑⵔⵐঠⵔ♂ⴑঠ

The next morning the girls woke up early after their first night sleeping in the RV. Their room was small, but adequate. There were plenty of drawers for all their clothes and they enjoyed being back with their grandparents.

Nelly the rag doll was resting comfortably on Megan's top bunk. They had had fun at Aunt Pat's and Uncle Rich's house, but it was nice being here where it was so quiet.

While they were eating breakfast, Grandpa came inside and handed Kendall a folded piece of paper. "I think this is for you two. It was stuck inside the door when I went out earlier this morning."

The girls unfolded the paper and recognized the symbols - Code Brown.

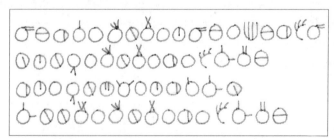

Megan got her journal and the girls decoded the message while their grandparents looked on.

## HEAD FOR THE BEACH STOP FOR A CLUE
## AT PONY TAILS LOOK FOR THE BLUE

"What is 'pony tails'? And what is 'the blue'?"
Megan wondered aloud. Grandma explained that Pony
Tails was the name of a store on the way to the beach.
Neither she nor Grandpa knew what "the blue" was.

"I guess you'll just have to go to Pony Tails and see
if you can see something blue, maybe a blue bike or a
blue car. It isn't far from here." He explained how to
get there from the campground.

The girls were excited as they got ready to go. They
carefully folded up their other messages from the boys
and Megan put them inside the front cover of her journal. She tucked it all down inside her backpack, put
that inside her bike basket, and the girls took off, heading for Pony Tails.

They found Pony Tails easily and parked their bicycles outside. They walked inside the store, not noticing
the two pairs of eyes following them. They roamed up
and down the aisles of Pony Tails, but didn't see anything that could be "the blue". They stopped for several
minutes and watched with fascination as the salt water
taffy machine rolled and stretched and cut and wrapped
candy, piece after mouthwatering piece. The young
woman behind the counter gave out samples. Delicious!

"We'll have to come back here sometime. I want to
get some of this candy to bring back to my parents.
They'd love it," Megan said.

Kendall agreed, then they remembered their mission
and took a second look around the store for something

blue. Somewhat discouraged, they returned to their bikes outside and then noticed a blue bandana tied to a post, near where they had parked their bicycles. "I didn't see that before, did you?" Kendall asked.

"No, we must have walked right past it. Do you think that's 'the blue'? " Megan said, smiling, as the excitement grew.          .

"Maybe. Let's untie it and see what it is."

The girls quickly untied the bandana and to their delight, found a new coded note inside. They sat down on a bench outside Pony Tails and Megan retrieved her journal and the girls quickly figured out their next clue:

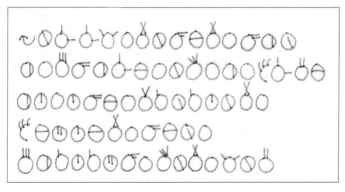

JOLLY ROGER HAS A WHALE OF A CLUE
AT THE VISITOR CENTER HES WAITING FOR YOU.

"Meg, we know where the Visitor Center is. We passed it when we went to the beach a few days ago, remember? Didn't this Pony Tails clue say something about going to the beach?"

"Yes, it said we have to head to the beach and stop here for a clue. So, I guess we need to keep heading to the beach and go to the Visitor Center. This is so fun," Megan said.

The girls bicycled across the causeway leaving Chincoteague behind. "Now I know why the other clue said, 'It's quite a hike, good thing you now have a bike.' This is a pretty far ride all the way to the beach," Kendall said.

They passed a long line of cars at the park entrance, cars loaded with families heading for the same beach. They pedaled silently along, noticing all sorts of strange birds perched at the water's edge. "I didn't see these before, did you?" Megan asked her cousin.

"No, I was too busy talking to Jack to pay much attention to what was outside. This is beautiful. Look at all that marsh. That must be the marsh grass that Ashley was telling us about. Hey, maybe we'll see some ponies!"

Ahead of them several cars were parked along the side of the road and people were standing in a group, many with cameras pointed out across the marsh. The girls got off their bikes and looked to see what the others were watching.

"Ponies! Look at the ponies!" Megan whispered in awe. "Wow, there are a whole bunch of them!"

The girls stood for several minutes entranced, watching the herd of ponies off in the distance, standing under the shade of a group of trees. Some of the ponies were brown, some spotted, and one was black. "Just think, in a few days, we're going to see them up close. I can't wait. They're beautiful," Kendall said, never taking her eyes off the ponies. Unknown to the girls, two pairs of eyes patiently watched them watching the ponies.

Finally, Kendall said, "I guess we should keep going. Remember, we're supposed to be on a treasure hunt."

"I feel like we just found the treasure," Megan said. "Those ponies are so cool. I could watch them all day."

"We can come back here later, okay? But we still have quite a ride to get to the beach. Let's go, and then stop here on the way back to the campground. How's that sound?"

"It sounds like something my mother would say," Megan said with a laugh.

"Sorry about that. I want to see them some more, too, but I want to see what else the boys have planned for us. We still have to figure out what the jolly roger is in the clue."

"I bet there's going to be a pirate flag someplace there, like the bandana, with another clue in it. Remember when Brian told us about the black pirate flags with the skulls on them? They probably made one. Okay, let's go and see if we can find it. The ponies will still be here later."

The girls got back on their bikes and rode all the way to the Tom's Cove Visitor Center and put their bicycles in the bike rack. They walked up the wooden walkway, checking for black flags as they went. The walkway continued past the information building and wound around the marsh. They walked a good distance, then stopped.

"I don't see anything out here. Maybe we should go inside. What do you think?" Megan asked.

Inside, the cool air conditioning was a welcome relief from the summer heat. The girls looked around the room but were concentrating on finding a jolly roger flag. The didn't see one. They browsed through the gift section, taking notice of many interesting books about ponies.

"Now that I've seen the ponies for real, I can't wait for the swim and auction next week. I see why everyone gets all excited about them. They're so pretty, and this whole place reminds me of the movie, 'Misty'," Megan said.

While they were standing in the gift area, a uniformed park ranger came up to them. "Can I help you girls with anything?" the man asked.

Startled, Kendall answered, "No, thank you. We're just looking around. Um, do you sell any flags in here?" she asked.

While Kendall was talking to the ranger, Megan looked at him. He was wearing brown pants and he had on a grey short-sleeved shirt with an emblem on the shoulder. But what caught her eye was a large whale tattooed on his left forearm. She felt a growing excitement, and looked at the man's name tag. Jonah Rogers it read. The man was friendly and nice, jolly, one could say! Hesitatingly, Megan said, "Excuse me, Mr. Rogers. Do you have a clue for us?"

Kendall was very surprised at Megan's question. Megan rarely spoke to strangers, and Kendall didn't understand why Megan was asking this man such a question.

"Why, yes, I do. You must be Megan." And turning to a speechless Kendall, he said, "And you're Kendall, I assume."

Kendall just nodded. The man turned to get something from behind the information counter. Kendall looked questioningly at her cousin. "Look at his tattoo. It's a whale. And his name is Jonah Rogers. He's Jolly Roger!" Megan said.

Kendall just laughed. "You crack me up, Megan. I didn't even notice the whale or his name tag. And I was the one standing here talking to him!"

Jolly Roger gave them their next clue. "Nice code, by the way. Very clever," he said with a smile. Big smiles were exchanged by the hidden observers, too.

The girls were seated outside on the wooden deck, right next to their bikes. They didn't even notice the streams of people going up and down the walkway that led to the Visitor Center. They had their code book out and were busy decoding their next message.

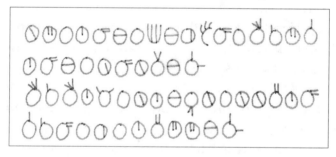

ON THE BEACH FIND THE SHOVEL
50 STEPS SOUTH DIG A TUNNEL

They hurriedly put everything into Megan's back-pack and rode to the edge of the parking lot, where they left their bikes and ran onto the beach. There was an amazingly large crowd of people on the beach, swimming, sunning, playing frisbee, and strolling at the water's edge.

"Shovel? How are we supposed to find a shovel here with all these people?" Kendall said.

"Beats me, but everything else has worked out okay. Let's just start walking and see what we find."

A few dozen steps onto the beach, they found an

empty sand pail and shovel. They looked at each other, then looked around to see if anyone seemed to be playing with it. There weren't any children close by. "This must be it. Now, we have to go 50 steps south. Which way is south?" Megan asked.

"That way, silly! We're on the Atlantic Ocean, which is east. You live that way," and she pointed in the opposite direction of the ocean. "So this way is north and that's south. Let's go!"

"...48, 49, 50! You think we should start digging here?" Kendall asked.

Megan looked around the area and found just what she thought she might see. "Kendall, over there." The girls ran to where Megan was pointing and there on the sand was a large "X" made of masking tape. "I guess 'X' marks the spot," she said with a laugh. "Let's dig!"

While the girls were digging with their hands, they didn't notice the other people around them. Suddenly, a pair of shadows cast dark lines right over where they were digging. "What are you looking for? Buried treasure?" said the shorter man. "Just need to know where to look." Then he laughed and continued walking.

"Leave them alone, stupid. We've got our own to worry about," said the taller man as they walked out of earshot.

"Megan, you know who those guys are? They're the pirates," Kendall whispered.

Suddenly Megan didn't feel much like digging any more.

"Hey, what did those guys say to you?" Brian asked, nearly out of breath from running. Jack joined him a few seconds later.

"I can't believe the pirates talked to you. What did

they say?" Jack asked.

"They asked what we're digging for, was it a buried treasure, and the shorter guy laughed. Then the taller guy -"

"Blackbeard," Brian interrupted.

"Yeah, Blackbeard told him to leave us alone and said they have their own to worry about, right, Meg?" Kendall said.

"I think that's what he said, but it was hard to hear. And Blackbeard called the other guy stupid."

"Their own what? Their own what to worry about? What else did they say?" Brian asked.

"That's all I heard. They kept walking, so it wasn't too easy to hear them," Kendall said.

"The one guy said something else, too. He said you just need to know where to look," Megan said.

"Where to look? Where to look for what? For a treasure?" Brian looked at Jack with concern. "These guys are starting to creep me out. They're showing up everywhere," he said. "Have you seen them any place else, besides when we saw them at the movies that night?"

"No, not until today," Kendall answered. "You haven't seen them either, have you, Megan?"

"No, I haven't. Not until today," she lied. She didn't want to have to tell the three of them about bumping into Blackbeard. She wished she'd already told Kendall about that, but if she told them now, it would be too embarrassing. He had called her an idiot. It was best to just not tell. What did it matter anyway?

"Those guys are up to something, but I don't know what yet. Let's all keep our eyes open for them, okay? If you see them, tell us, and if we see them, we'll tell you. Maybe we can get Ashley to watch out for them, too," Brian said.

"Hey, how about finishing your digging, guys," Jack said to his cousins.

"Oh, yeah, I almost forgot what we were doing here," Kendall laughed.

She and Megan continued their digging and a few minutes later they uncovered a small plastic bag. They pulled it out of the deep hole and brushed off the sand.

"Cute. We saw these in one of the stores. This is perfect, you guys," Kendall said as she opened the bag and took out the two small, stuffed ponies. She held one out to Megan, who grinned as she gently touched the pony.

"Thanks, you guys, this is a perfect treasure."

The foursome walked back to the parking lot where there were now four bicycles. "We've been following you all day, ever since you left the campground," Jack explained proudly.

"Really? We didn't see you," Kendall said, amazed.

"Good. Then we did it just right," Brian said. "Let's ride to Muller's and have some ice cream and you two can tell us about the treasure you're going to hide for us!"

"I'll never tell," Kendall laughed.

"My lips are sealed!" Megan agreed with a smile.

# CHAPTER 13

## PONIES

Brian was becoming more suspicious of the pirates, or booters, as Jack liked to call them, with each passing hour. He and Jack took a bike ride out to the Visitor Center to see Jonah Rogers, the park ranger.

"Yes, I've seen those two fellows around several times in the past day or so. They keep coming in and looking at our books and maps and asking questions about the island. I imagine this is their first time to Assateague. We get an awful lot of visitors here in the summer," Jonah said.

"But were they acting weird, or strange or anything?" Brian asked.

"Not that I noticed, why?"

"They're booters, freebooters. You know, pirates," Jack said to a very surprised Jonah.

Brian explained quickly, "It's not that they're really pirates, but they're part of our game. We've just been seeing them around a lot and wondered what they're up to, that's all."

"Well, I'm glad to see that you kids are having such a good time with the pirate game." He leaned his head closer to them. "And how about that other matter we talked about?" he asked, lowering his voice.

"When we find it, you'll be the first to know," Brian

whispered.

Back outside, they thought about their next move. "I didn't want to tell Jonah why I really want to know about those guys, but I think they're after our treasure," Brian said.

"Our treasure? You mean the Wilson treasure?"

"What other treasure are we looking for, man? Why else would they be here. And think about the stuff they bought. A shovel? What's that for?"

"Brian, I think you've gone a little nutsy over this pirate thing. Those guys are probably here working on someone's house and needed a shovel to dig a hole. That's not so unusual, is it?"

"Well, I just don't want anyone else to find the Wilson treasure, just us."

"I wish you'd let me tell the girls about it. They could probably be a big help. Did you see how smart Kendall is about those coins? And Megan always has good ideas."

Brian thought for a moment. "They can help. They can help us by keeping an eye on those dudes. We can tell them it's just part of our game, but they might be able to help us keep one step ahead of them."

Grandma and Grandpa Bayley had a big day lined up for the girls. Their first stop was the Beebe Ranch. There the girls saw the actual horse, Misty. It had been stuffed and preserved for generations to see.

"This house doesn't look the same as the house in the movie, Grandpa," Megan said as they left.

"That's because this is the house that the grandfather's son lived in. This is the real farm where Misty lived," he explained. "And tonight, we're going to see more ponies, real Chincoteague ponies, and you can even ride one if you'd like."

"Really?" Megan said. "Are we going to Assateague to where they've rounded up the ponies for tomorrow's swim?"

"No, honey," Grandpa laughed. "We're going to the Pony Center tonight to see a pony show."

"That sounds great!" Kendall said, and her cousin quickly agreed. Grandpa decided to take a quick drive to Assateague to see if they could see the ponies being rounded up by the firemen on horseback. As they passed the Visitor Center, Megan noticed a black truck parked outside. She tapped Kendall on the arm and pointed to the truck and mouthed the word, "pirates" to her. Kendall nodded in understanding.

The kids had all agreed to meet at Muller's at 3:00 for an ice cream cone to discuss their plans for the pony swim and auction events. The girls arrived a few minutes early and quietly tucked a note in their secret hiding place.

Brian and Jack walked into Muller's dining room, took a quick look around, and flipped open the chimney door. "I knew there would be some mail in here for us," Brian teased.

As the other three enjoyed their frozen treats, Brian decoded the message:

PIRATE SHIP DOCKED AT JONAHS PLACE.

"Is this one of our clues?" he asked.

"No, silly, you asked us to keep an eye out for the pirates. So we did, and we just saw them at the Visitor Center about an hour ago," Megan said.

Brian felt the knot in his stomach twist. He was con-

vinced, now more than ever, that those men were after
his treasure. He now thought of the Wilson treasure as
his, and he was determined to get there first.

"So, when do we get our first clue to find our treasure?" Jack asked.

"We have to find some time to work on that. Be patient. We're supposed to be having a nice, quiet beach
vacation, remember?" Kendall said to Jack.

"Yeah, yeah, I know, but we did your treasure hunt
so now it's our turn to look," Jack said.

"You're right, Jack, it is our turn to look for a treasure!" Brian said with a wink.

Back at the RV, Megan and Kendall were trying to
figure out where to hide the boys' treasures. Kendall
looked around their tiny room. Her eyes rested on
Megan's tan bag, purchased at the yard sale. "Let's put
the stuff in your bag. Then we can just put the bag anyplace, but they'll never think to look inside it. We could
bring it to the pony swim tomorrow with our lunch in it
and then later, we can put their stuff inside, and still
have the bag with us. It'll be funny when they realize
that their treasure has been right under their noses all
the time!"

Megan thought again about telling Kendall about
her encounter with Blackbeard, but decided not to. She
still felt embarrassed every time she thought about it
and there was no reason to bring it up. "Sure, the bag
will be fine. You're right, they'll never guess it's in
there," Megan said.

After dinner Grandpa had a little surprise for each of
the girls. "Your grandfather loves finding just the right
thing for someone. And you two are very special.

We're having such a nice summer with you," Grandma said. "It's almost like having your mothers here again, like when they were children."

Grandpa presented each girl with a copy of "Misty" and a small camera. "I was at the Kite Koop today and saw these books. I thought you both might like a copy. And you'll need a camera to take pictures of the pony swim in the morning and the auction the next day. You can put them into scrapbooks of your adventures this summer."

The day ended pleasantly with the pony show at the Chincoteague Pony Center. Megan and Kendall cheered as the beautiful ponies performed tricks. Afterward, both girls rode horseback for the first time. It was a day to remember. As Megan closed her eyes, she looked at her little stuffed pony that the boys had given her. "Treasure," she said. A perfect name for her pony.

CHAPTER 14
# THE SWIM

Thinking back on it later, Megan would wonder if anyone on Chincoteague Island slept at all that night. With thousands of people on the island waiting to see the famous ponies swim, the excitement had been building for days. And because the swim itself would last for only a few minutes, there were going to be huge crowds of people all hoping to catch a glimpse of the ponies swimming the channel. Several hours before daybreak, the town was swarming with people armed with cameras, folding beach chairs, and snacks. Ashley came to the campground and met the girls early, very early, about 4:30 in the morning. Ashley was a veteran of many pony swims and knew that they had to go early in order to beat the crowd. The three bicycled to a spot at Memorial Park that Ashley knew would be the perfect spot from which to see the ponies swim across the channel. The crowd of people grew until it seemed to be a sea of children and adults, all waiting patiently for the arrival of the famous ponies.

"This is so much fun. I can't believe there are so many people," Megan said.

"And we can only see some of the people from here," Ashley said. "Thousands of people from all over the country are packed onto this island. I'm surprised it doesn't sink!" The girls laughed. "Really, right now the causeway is bumper to bumper and there are buses carrying people all over Chincoteague. This is the busiest day of the year, and everyone will try to get at least a peek at the ponies. Do you see the boats out there?" She pointed to several of the larger boats crowding the channel on either side of the path left clear for the ponies. "There are people from newspapers from all over, and TV stations, too, out there. Later on, there might even be a helicopter with cameramen shooting the swim. I guess you two didn't realize just how big a deal this swim is," she said, noting the amazed looks on the cousins' faces.

The girls waited patiently as the firemen over on Assateague calmed the corraled ponies, who seemed to know what was about to happen. The ponies had been swimming over on this day each year since before Grandpa was born.

At the appointed time, when the currents were calm and the tide slack and safe, the firemen on horseback guided the herd of nearly two hundred ponies into the water at the edge of Assateague Island. The ponies first walked into the water, then about twenty feet out, when their feet no longer touched the bottom, they swam. Mothers and foals, big and small, all walked into the salty water of the channel. One by one, their noses were stuck up in the air and their bodies disappeared under the water until all you could see of them was their heads, with ears pricked forward, and a bit of their manes. They swam like dogs, their powerful legs pumping up and down. Behind some, you could see their tails floating on the surface of the water. Some of the foals got tired of swimming and rested their heads on their mother's hind quarters, hitching a ride across the channel.

As the ponies went in the water, the crowd on the Chincoteague side of the channel swelled with cheers. "They hit the water!" "Here they come!" "Watch the ponies!" Small children were watching, perched on their parents' shoulders. As the dark pool of ponies moved across the channel, the cheering became louder and louder. Megan and Kendall watched intently, both worried about the small foals swimming for their first time in the chilly waters.

"Look, over there, that one looks like Misty," Megan said, pointing out a light colored pony making its way across the water. "They're so little!"

"There's a black one," Kendall said, pointing at the small pony that seemed to be ahead of most of the other small ones. "Does that one look like Star?" she asked.

Ashley looked to where Kendall was pointing. "Yes, it does. It has the same mark on its forehead. Cool!"

"I'd name that one Midnight if it was my horse," Kendall said.

"I like that little tan one," Megan said, pointing out the Misty lookalike. "I'm going to call her Treasure."

Finally, when the first ponies hit the shore on Chincoteague, the firemen made a ring around them so that the crowd of spectators couldn't get too close. The girls managed to stand just behind the firemen and were able to get a good look at the ponies as they came up on land, shaking out the cool water from their fur. A dozen or more full grown ponies of all colors were shaking and prancing, excited by all the noise and the people straining to get a look at them. Then, the first foal to reach the shore emerged quickly from the water

and ran to stand beside its mother. It was the black colt
with a white star on its forehead and he had four white
stockings. His wet coat was shiny in the sun and looked
almost a glossy purple. "Midnight was first! He's the
first foal out," Kendall said. She turned to Ashley.
"That means he's King Neptune, right?" she asked.

"It sure does. Your Midnight's King Neptune, and
he'll spend the day in his own special pen. And he
looks a lot like Star." The girls watched each pony
climb up out of the waters of Chincoteague Channel
and rejoin the herd. Midnight, with his mother, was led
to one side. Later, he would be receiving congratulations from hundreds of children as he waited to be raf-
fled off and adopted by a new family. The entire herd
of ponies came to rest on the shore, mothers keeping a
very close watch on their babies. Megan was over-
whelmed at the sight of nearly two hundred ponies
standing so close by. And she was not alone in her feelings. The crowd of spectators had quieted down and
were watching the tired ponies in awe. It was a once in
a lifetime experience for thousands of people.

While the ponies were resting, Ashley and the
cousins made their way through the crowds of people,
pushing their bicycles in and out until they were finally
able to ride. They took a short cut to Main Street and
joined hundreds of other people already there, waiting
for another glimpse of the famous ponies. Ashley got
the girls settled into a good spot, then jogged over to
Muller's to check on her work schedule for the day.
With so many people in town, she knew that she would
be needed to help scoop cool ice cream all day long, especially on such a hot day. She returned a short time
later.

"This is a good spot. We'll be able to see the ponies run down Main Street from here. I come here every year to watch, and it's always exciting. It's quite a sight, so many horses all together. That's what makes Chincoteague famous!" A few minutes later Ashley turned her head to look up Main Street, which was now as crowded as Memorial Park had been just a short time earlier. "Do you hear that?" Ashley asked. The girls listened. Off in the distance they could hear a clopping sound and voices raised in cheer. "They're on their way!"

Megan was unprepared for the event that was about to unfold. A roaring sound grew as the ponies came closer. People were standing shoulder to shoulder, pushing forward to see when the ponies came by. Video cameras were poised to catch every movement. Megan and Kendall had their cameras ready, too. Then, like a gigantic parade, a huge thundering noise, like a dark storm cloud, rolled into view. Wild ponies, kept in a tight herd by horseback firemen, trotted and ran, their hooves making a deafening sound on the hard pavement of Main Street. Megan strained forward, hoping to catch a glimpse of Treasure. Indeed, there she was, running along side of her mother, just feet from where Megan and her friends were standing. Kendall was looking for Midnight, but didn't see him. Two hundred horses passed by within a few minutes, the crowd yelling and cheering the entire time. Then, at the very end of the herd, came a tight group of horseback firemen, surrounding a small black colt and his mother. "Midnight!" Kendall said. A voice coming from a loud speaker announced King Neptune's arrival. The crowd cheered with delight.

When the ponies had turned off Main Street onto the carnival grounds, the crowd began to break up and the volume of sound dropped. "That was amazing. I can't believe this. I just wish my mom could be here," Megan said.

"Our moms came here when they were our age and did see the ponies, Megan," Kendall said.

"Really? I wonder why she never said anything about it. I'll never forget this, as long as I live."

The girls were exhausted from the sheer excitement of the morning, and because they got up so early. They went back to the campground and shared all the news with Grandma and Grandpa.

"You should have been there, Grandma," Megan said. "It was amazing. The ponies are beautiful. I saw the cutest little one. I named her Treasure, and she looks like Misty."

Grandma smiled. "I've seen those ponies many, many times, and each time it's exciting all over again." She looked at Megan. "Why don't you write some of this into your journal now, while it's still fresh in your mind, and you can tell your parents all about it when you get home."

"Yeah, and write about Midnight and the treasure hunt the boys had for us, too," Kendall added. "I think I'll start reading 'Misty'. I guess this is about the perfect day to read it, don't you think?"

"Can't think of a better one," Grandpa said as he looked proudly at his granddaughters, then smiled at Grandma.

## Chapter 15
# Suspicions

⊙ꙶⓓⓞꙘꙶⓄꙶꙌꙶⓑⓞꙶⓄ ꙶⓜⓘ

That evening, Megan and Kendall invited Maddie to go with them to the carnival. There, they met Ashley, Jack, and Brian. The boys were introduced to Maddie and fingerspelled their words as best they could.

Brian pointed to the ferris wheel, then pointed to Maddie and spelled, "R-I-D-E?" Maddie smiled and nodded and sat between Brian and Jack, with the other three girls in the next seat. Up, up, up in the air they went, giving them a terrific view of Chincoteague.

Jack was the first to spot them. "Booters, over there," he said to Brian, pointing down by a snack booth. Brian followed his finger and saw them, Blackbeard and Billy Blads. Maddie looked on.

"We can't get away from these guys. Everywhere we go, there they are," Brian said.

"Maybe they're following us," Jack said, teasing.

Brian considered the idea. "You might be right. We need to watch them and see what they do."

Maddie turned her head back and forth, watching each boy as he spoke. She tapped Brian on the arm and pointed to the men they had been talking about. "W-H-O?" she spelled.

"P-I-R-A-T-E," Brian answered.

Maddie knew about their pirate game from Megan,

so she nodded with understanding. But she kept her
eyes on the men as the ride continued around and
around. After the children got off the ferris wheel, they
wandered around, stopping for hot dogs and drinks,
then waited in line for another ride. While the boys
were busy watching a young man juggle, Kendall and
Megan handed Ashley a folded note and asked her to
put the paper on Brian's bicycle early the next morning.
It was their first clue to find the treasure the girls had
hidden for them.

Maddie had been watching the pirates as best she
could as the happy group enjoyed the carnival festivities. She saw them sitting down on a bench eating
pizza. Maddie nudged Brian and looked at the men.
Brian followed where she was looking and saw the
backs of the two pirates. Maddie motioned for Brian to
follow her, and the two of them slipped away from their
friends and stood right behind the men. With so much
activity on the carnival grounds, the pirates didn't even
notice the kids behind him. Brian listened.

"This is going to be easy. Like taking candy from a
baby," Billy Blads said.

"Stupid, it isn't as easy as you think. We're not the
only people with the same idea, I'm sure. We have to be
the first, and remember, we're here to make Mr. Wilson
happy."

"Yeah, make Mr. Wilson happy. He's going to be
happy alright. Real happy," Blads said, and laughed.

Brian's stomach nearly did a flip and he moved
away before he made a noise and alerted the pirates of
his presence. Now he knew for sure they were after the
Wilson treasure, his treasure. Maddie wanted to know
what he heard, but he wasn't able to tell her. He needed

Megan to tell Maddie, and to do that, he'd need to tell Megan and Kendall about the Wilson treasure. Oh, well, he thought. He might as well tell them. Maybe Jack was right and they could help after all.

"Ten chests of gold and silver and stuff? And it's buried on Assateague and no one has ever found it? And you didn't tell us until now?" Kendall said. She was furious with both boys. "Why didn't you tell us? I thought we were all doing this pirate thing together."

Brian tried to explain, but he didn't manage to calm Kendall down much. In fairness to his best friend, he said, "Jack wanted me to tell you from the beginning. He asked me to tell you several times, so you can be mad at me, but don't be mad at Jack. It's all my fault."

Megan was busy trying to sign to Maddie and let her know what was being said.

"I thought you said those guys are repairing someone's house," Kendall said, still angry.

"Well, I just made that up. I've been suspicious of them ever since we first saw them," Brian said.

"So, you lied about that and were keeping secrets from us. Great. And I thought we were all friends." Kendall moved away from the group.

Megan thought about her secret and felt badly. She wished she had already told her friends about it. She decided to look at the paper Blackbeard dropped and see if it had anything on it that might help Brian and Jack find their treasure. Then, she'd tell them about her encounter with the pirate.

That night just before bed, Megan opened her red leather journal and pulled out the folded pony flyer and turned it over. The name "Wilson" was written on it and a cryptic map was drawn with brief notations scratched in.  After the lights went out, Megan laid awake for a long time, picturing the pirate's map and remembering her encounter with Blackbeard.  She thought about how angry Kendall was going to be when she found out Megan had been keeping a secret from her.  She finally fell asleep and had fitful dreams all night long of pirates chasing her and her friends.

CHAPTER 16
# THE AUCTION

⊙♂⊖⊙⊙♂♂⊙♭⊙♡⊕

T he next day started early once again. Ashley and the girls left on their bicycles and headed for the carnival grounds to get a good spot for the auction. Maddie was with them. Grandma and Grandpa planned to meet them down there later on. Ashley assured the girls that the boys would get their note. She had put it on Brian's bicycle just before she left, and she had seen no activity yet at Aunt Pat's and Uncle Rich's house.

While the girls waited for the auction to begin, the Kellam household was getting ready to join them. Aunt Pat had gotten a call from someone at the Chamber office saying that there was a broken water pipe and a big mess to clean up. The office would be closed until later that afternoon, so Aunt Pat had the day off to go to the pony auction. She and Uncle Rich would join Mr. and Mrs. Walker at the annual auction. The boys had made it clear the night before that they would go on their own and meet up with the girls and their grandparents at the carnival grounds. With such a big crowd of people descending on one corner of town for the auction, it was possible that they wouldn't see each other until later in the day.

The Kellams and Walkers joined hundreds of other families as they assembled for the auction. The firemen

and volunteers began to bring up the foals, one at a
time. The crowd cheered for each pony, then quieted
down as the bidding began. As each pony was sold, a
huge cheer rose up again, and the pony was led back to
the pen.

"Pat, nice we got to come to the auction, isn't is?"
her friend, Dorothy, said.

"Yes, I guess you got the same call. Yesterday I was
disappointed knowing that I would miss the auction.
But now, here we are."

"I'm glad too, but it does seem strange that they'd
shut down the whole Chamber office just because of
some broken water pipes. Pony auction day is always
busy there. I can't imagine the line of people waiting
when we reopen this afternoon," Dorothy said.

"Well, I'm just glad I got to come today. Did you see
that last pony that sold? She was beautiful."

Across the ring, Megan stood watching with her
friends. The ponies were so cute, just like in the movie
"Misty". But in the back of her mind, Megan was turning over the cryptic note scratched on the back of the
paper she had found at the yard sale. She took a deep
breath and decided the time had come to tell Kendall
and not hold on to the secret any longer.

To her great relief, Kendall was not mad. "Megan, I
know those guys give you the creeps. I wish you had
told me before, so you wouldn't have to worry about it.
What a jerk, calling you names, when it was his fault he
bumped into you. And I can't believe he stole that tan
bag from the yard sale. Can you imagine?"

Megan told Kendall about the notes on the paper,
too, and that the name "Wilson" was there.

"We need to tell the boys. So, those guys are after

the Wilson treasure, just like Brian thought. Let's see if we can find them."

Megan explained what was going on to Maddie as best she could. Maddie seemed to understand Megan's concern about the pirates. Maddie didn't like the looks of those men at all. The girls moved through the crowd, looking for the boys, when an idea struck Megan. She tried to call to Kendall, but with the noisy cheers for the ponies, Kendall didn't hear her. Instead, Megan tapped Maddie on the arm and signed to her, "I'm going to the RV. I have to check something. Tell Kendall," and with that, she was off.

Megan found her bike where she had left it, along with rows of other bicycles. Maddie had a bike with her, so they had all ridden together. With the crowds in town, a bike was much faster than Ashley's truck for getting around. Something Grandpa had said kept repeating itself inside Megan's head and she just had to be sure.

Meanwhile, Jack and Brian had gotten their first clue from the girls, stuck between the spokes of Brian's bicycle. They decoded the message which read:

THE COLOR TO LOOK FOR IS TAN MAN.

"That's a strange clue. Tan what?" Jack asked.

"Beats me, but we have to keep our eyes open for something tan, man!" Brian said as they hopped on their bicycles and made their way through the sea of people walking to the carnival grounds for the auction. Surprisingly, the first people they saw when they got there were Jack's parents and Aunt Pat and Uncle Rich.

"Aunt Pat, what are you doing here? Playing hooky from work? I thought you were working at the Chamber office today," Jack said to his aunt.

"I got lucky and got the day off. There are some broken pipes so someone called and said they're closing the office until the afternoon. The office is closed, which is perfect. Now I can be here and see the ponies."

"Closed, perfect," Brian repeated, knowing that he had heard that somewhere before. Then, it struck him. "Jack, we have to find the girls," he said, and started weaving through the crowd on his bicycle. Jack didn't know why Brian was in such a rush, but followed him as best he could.

A short time later, breathless from riding, running, and pushing his bicycle with one good arm, Brian spotted Kendall. "There you are. I've been looking all over for you. We've got trouble, big trouble," Brian said in a tumble of words. "Hey, where's Megan?"

Kendall and Ashley looked around and noticed, for the first time, that Megan wasn't with them. They started to call for her, but Maddie stopped them. "RV" she fingerspelled to Kendall.

"RV? She's at the campground? Why isn't she with you?" Brian asked.

Kendall explained to the boys about Megan's secret encounter with Blackbeard and that she had found a paper with "Wilson" and some other notes written on it.

Brian took charge. "You girls go to the campground and see if you can find Megan. We're going there, too, but we're taking a different way. We'll all meet there. And if you see the pirates, be careful," he said. And with that, he was off, Jack following closely behind.

## CHAPTER 17
# THE BRIDGE

Megan was hidden behind a bush, her backpack clutched to her chest to calm her pounding heart. She had remembered Grandpa saying that the treasure coins were very valuable and hoped that they were well guarded. She also remembered Brian saying that pirates attacked targets that were weak or poorly protected. After looking at the paper once again, Megan concluded that the pirates were going to steal the treasure coins and she had rushed to the Chamber office. Once she arrived, she had seen the "Closed" sign on the door and thought it was odd for the office to be closed on such a busy day. Then she remembered one more thing, that Brian had overhead the pirates talking in the hardware store and they said, "Closed. Perfect," and laughed. Megan just knew they had put up the closed sign. She could hear strange noises coming from the building and spotted their black truck not far away. Maybe she had listened to too many of her mother's mysteries, but she knew what she had to do.

Megan quietly unzipped her backpack and pulled out her tan bag, the one filled with the boys' treasures. We can hide them later, she thought. She reached to the bottom and found her camera. With care, she aimed the camera at the truck and took a picture of the license auction, she thought. There were still plenty left on the roll. Then she stood up and edged close to a window. She heard glass break and sat back down, then moved away from the building, still hidden but frightened. Just then, some movement not far away caught her attention. It was Brian and Jack, both crouched down, hiding just as she was.

Megan made sure the boys were watching, then told them what was happening inside the building. "P-I-R-A-T-E-S S-T-E-A-L-I-N-G C-O-I-N-S," she finger-spelled slowly. Both boys understood and nodded.

"G-E-T H-E-L-P," Megan pleaded.

The boys whispered and then Jack slowly stood up. As he moved slowly toward his bike, he noticed the tan bag Megan had left on the ground. He remembered their clue, "The color to look for is tan, man," smiled, and picked it up.

Just then, there was a loud crash and the kids saw Blackbeard drop a bag out a small open window. It was a tan bag, and it landed behind a bush, exactly where Megan had been just moments before. Suddenly, the door opened and Billy Blads came out, wearing work gloves. He looked around for the bag and saw Jack, tan bag over his shoulder, riding on his bike away from the building, going for help. Blackbeard came out a few seconds later, also wearing gloves, and Blads yelled to him, "The kid's got the bag," and raced off after Jack.

Blackbeard looked at the bush underneath the small window. "I'll wait here," Blackbeard said, then, as soon as Billy Blads was a short distance away, running after Jack as fast as he could, Blackbeard grabbed the bag from behind the bush and ran to his truck. "Idiot," he said, and laughed.

As soon as the black truck pulled away, Megan breathed for the first time in what seemed an hour. Brian, who had remained hidden, came over to where she was. "I'll go get help. You go back to the campground and stay there," and he was gone. She saw a streak of orange as he raced off on his bike, cast in the air.

Megan suddenly remembered the drawbridge at the entrance to Chincoteague Island and got back to the campground and their RV as fast as she could. She was relieved to find Maddie, Kendall, and Ashley waiting for her. Megan told them what had happened as quickly as she could, her hands flying as she tried to keep Maddie informed. Words tumbled out. "The pirates stole the coins, one is chasing Jack, Brian went for help, and we have to get the bridge opened." She was on the edge of panic as she recalled Billy Blads chasing after Jack, just like in her dream last night.

Kendall stayed calm and said they needed to find a police officer. With so many people around town, that didn't seem like a very difficult thing to do. And sure enough, within minutes they spotted a policeman at the entrance to the campground. As calmly as she could, Kendall told the officer that they needed help, that pirates stole the coins from the Chamber of Commerce building, and that they needed to open the bridge to trap the pirates so they couldn't leave the island.

Much to their dismay, the man laughed. "Pirates, you say? You kids have fun, now, you hear?" and got in his police car and left.

They stood there for a moment, wondering what to do next. Panic was thick in the air as all the girls were worried about Jack. Just then, Grandpa drove up.

"There you are. Been looking for you. Want some lunch?" he asked.

Without a word of explanation, the four girls yanked open the car doors and piled in. "We have to get the bridge opened," Megan said. "Hurry, Grandpa! Please."

As he drove toward the bridge, Ashley guided him through all her short cuts. Traffic was moving slowly because of all the people in town for the auction. On the way, the girls tried to fill Grandpa in on the pirate situation. He understood that they weren't playing a game, and was there to help.

Jack rode his bike as fast as he could, considering all the people in the way. He zigged and zagged between them, much as he did on roller skates. His heart pounded as he heard Blads yelling at him from a short distance behind. "I'm going to kill you, kid, if you don't give me that bag," Blads said.

Jack was so startled to hear the man mention Megan's bag, he nearly lost his balance. Why would he want her bag, he wondered to himself. But Jack was determined not only to get away from this pirate, but to catch him as well. He was thinking about stories Brian had told him about pirates and smiled to himself as he hatched his plan. He slowed down slightly and changed direction and looked over his shoulder to make sure Billy Blads was still in pursuit. He was.

Grandpa's car was on Main Street, edging its way to the bridge. Suddenly he stopped and told the girls to get out and run to the bridge. It would be faster. They all got out and started running up the road when up ahead of them, the bridge magically began to open, bringing all traffic on Chincoteague to a dead standstill.

Before they could even wonder how or why it opened, Brian ran up with a uniformed man close behind. Megan and Kendall recognized Jolly Roger, the park ranger.

"Jonah called the bridge and they opened it up. Are we in time? Where's Blackbeard? Where's Jack and Billy Blads?" Brian asked quickly.

"Hey, guys, over here," Jack called to his friends. "Where's Blackbeard? I got Billy Blads marooned out there," and he pointed to a small boat floating in the water near the bridge.

"What happened to him?" Brian asked, laughing as he saw the pirate struggling to paddle the boat with his hands.

"He chased me right to where I knew there was an old boat, no oars or anything. He was yelling about your bag, Megan," he said, turning to Megan, "so I tossed the bag into the boat as bait, and he took it," Jack finished, beaming.

"Dude, you're awesome. Now, we just need to find Blackbeard. He's got the Knight Rider and all the other coins."

At the bridge, the police officer the girls had tried to enlist to help them, jumped out of his car. "The Chamber building was broken into. What do you know about this?" he asked the children.

"The guy with the coins is in a black pickup truck, license plate BTB 1724," Brian said.

"He has the coins in a tan bag that has a black mark on the side. It looks like that one down there in the boat," and Megan pointed to where Billy Blads was still struggling to get ashore. "I even have pictures of everything," and she handed the officer her small camera.

Meanwhile, Jonah and the bridge operator had gotten down onto a fishing boat and were near Billy Blads and his small boat. "Need a hand, sir?" Jonah asked.

Blads gladly got onto the fishing boat, shaking, and Jonah picked up the tan bag. A police officer who had been hiding in the boat cabin came out and snapped hand cuffs onto the pirate.

"We've got the bag, so you better tell us everything," Jonah said. "Where's your partner?"

Billy Blads spilled everything. He told them about his partner, Fred Hanson, and the man they worked for, Mr. Wilson. The police officer radioed for help and told them to look for Hanson.

Jonah and the police officer got Billy Blads, or Williams, off the boat and onto shore. The group of onlookers, Brian and Jack, Grandpa, and the girls, were all there. "Hey, jerk," Brian said to Billy Blads. "Your partner double crossed you. He has the coins." And with that, Jonah handed Brian the tan bag.

"Let me open it, can I?" Megan asked. Brian handed her the bag. She opened it and pulled out the pirate book and several small pirate figures. She handed them to the boys. "Here's your treasure. Sorry we didn't get to hide it!"

"Cool, this is the book from 1724," Brian said, opening the cover of the pirate book. "Now I have my own copy."

"Thanks for the treasures, girls," Jack said. "Funny how a pirate almost stole them, huh?" and he laughed.

"Mr. Wilson, I got the coins. Everything's fine. Williams? He went running after some kid. No big loss there. He's a complete idiot. Next time, I'm leaving

him out. I'm stuck in traffic with all the pony junk, but
I'll be there as soon as I can. I'll give you a call when
I'm back on the highway." Blackbeard clicked off his
cell phone and turned on the radio. He was whistling,
feeling quite pleased with himself. He didn't hear the
knocking on his window. Suddenly, the truck door was
opened and two police officers pulled him out of the
truck and snapped on the hand cuffs. "Hey, what are
you doing? What's going on here?" he yelled.

"I see what we need, right there," the officer said
and picked up the tan bag, the one with the black mark
on it, from the floor of the truck.

"There must be some mistake, officers. I'm here for
the pony auction. No hard feelings, if you'll just give
me my bag back, and I'll be on my way."

"First, you'll probably want to have a word with
your friend, Billy Williams. Sure is a talkative guy," the
officer said.

"Idiot," Blackbeard said.

Daniel Ashford arrived and confirmed that all of his
coins were there in the tan bag. After speaking with the
police for over an hour, the children, along with
Grandpa, went to Muller's for an ice cream cone. Just to
settle their nerves, of course.

Without a second thought, Brian opened the chimney cupboard and pulled out a note.

"I forgot we put that in there, so much has happened," Kendall said.

Everyone watched as Brian and Jack decoded their
final message:

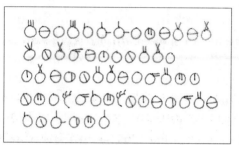

## WE WILL NEVER FORGET OUR TREASURE HUNT
## ON CHINCOTEAGUE ISLAND

"That's for sure!" Megan said, and they all burst out laughing.

"So, Brian, tell us more about 'our' Wilson treasure," Kendall said. "And this time, I want all the details!"

*The End*

# Author's Note

The story and the characters in **Treasure On Chincoteague Island** are fictional, but it takes place in very real locations. Chincoteague and Assateague Islands in Virginia are located off the coast of the narrow stretch of land known as the Virginia Eastern Shore. This rural and historic piece of land is connected to the rest of the state by a 17 mile-long bridge tunnel at the south end and is connected to Maryland at the north.

Pirates were active in this region for many years, and the treasures described, the Charles Wilson treasure and the Beale treasure, are factual. Blackbeard did use Assateague as one of his hideouts, and some of his descendents still live in the area. For further information about pirates, read **A General History of the Robberies and Murders of the Most Notorius Pirates** by Captain Charles Johnson, first published in 1724.

The coins described in the story are real as well. For further information about these and other coins, contact Treasures of Maryland, PO Box 1275, Salisbury, MD 21802 or treasuresofmaryland@comcast.net.

This is the second book in a series. The characters were introduced in the first book, **The Hidden Key**. For further information about this and my other books, visit us on the web: www.sheepdogpress.com.

# CODE BROWN

This is the code that Megan invented for her friends to use. Look at the Fingerspelling Alphabet on the next page and see if you can discover the connection between the two alphabets. Then, try to write your own secret messages in Code Brown. Maybe you can even make up your own code like Megan did.

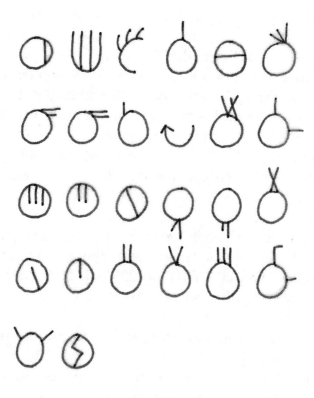

# FINGERSPELLING ALPHABET

Megan knew how to fingerspell because she knew Sign Language. Fingerspelling is part of Sign Language. Fingerspelling is used to spell out names of people and places, and can be used when you don't know the sign for a word. Practice spelling your name with the alphabet below. Hold your "spelling" hand so that the palm of your hand faces away from you and toward the person who is "reading" your fingerspelling.

## WRITING IN CODE

Practice writing in code using Megan's Code Brown.
Write the symbols beneath each of the following lines.
Make a copy of Code Brown for a friend, and you two
can trade secret messages!

My name is _____

I live in _____

My favorite color is _____

I LIKE TO READ.

I CAN MAKE MY

OWN SECRET

CODE.

*Hint: Don't forget to put a small circle between words.*

# MAKE YOUR OWN CODE

Try your hand at making up your own secret code.  Use
the space below to write a symbol next to each letter of
the alphabet.  When you are finished, make up a name
for your code!

| A | H | O | V |
|---|---|---|---|
| B | I | P | W |
| C | J | Q | X |
| D | K | R | Y |
| E | L | S | Z |
| F | M | T |   |
| G | N | U |   |

The name of my code is _____.

# CAN YOU FIND THESE PLACES?

If you visit Chincoteague Island and the surrounding areas, check off all the places you can find that were in the story.

☐ THE DREAM ROLLER RINK

☐ NASA WALLOPS FLIGHT FACILITY

☐ MULLER'S OLD FASHIONED ICE CREAM PARLOUR

☐ ISLAND ROXY THEATER

☐ SHOWARD BROTHERS HARDWARE

☐ MISS MOLLY'S

☐ KITE KOOP BOOKSTORE

☐ PONY TAILS

☐ CHAMBER OF COMMERCE

☐ TOM'S COVE VISITOR CENTER

☐ CHINCOTEAGUE PONY CENTER

☐ MEMORIAL PARK

☐ BEEBE RANCH

# SIGN LANGUAGE

Megan and Maddie communicated in Sign Language, the language of the deaf. Sign Language uses the hands, the face, and body movements to communicate. People who sign are able to "say" everything to each other that people who talk do, just in a different way. Many deaf people can also "lipread". By watching the speaker's mouth, they can understand some or all of what the person is saying. When signing and finger-spelling, it is important to first maintain "eye contact" with your partner and do not block their view of your face. When you practice the signs below and on the following pages, you may want to mouth the words at the same time as you are signing. Try practicing in a mirror. Happy signing!

**Mother**
*Tap your thumb on your chin.*

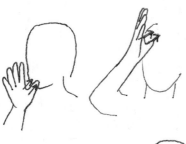

**Father**
*Tap your thumb on your fore-head.*

**Eat**
*Touch tips of fingers and thumb together; move in front of mouth like feeding.*

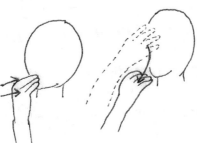

**Sleep**
*Put open hand in front of face, then move down and away from face, closing hand.*

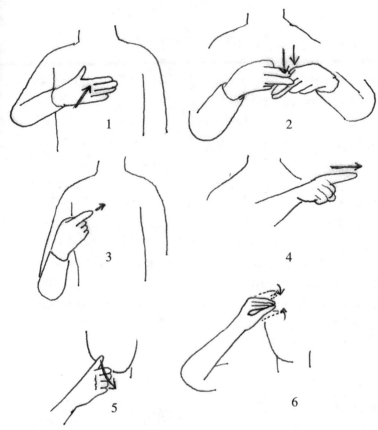

1. **My**       *Place an open, flat hand on your chest.*

2. **Name**     *Make the letter "h" with both hands. Tap right "h" on top of left "h".*

3. **Me**       *Point to yourself with index finger extended.*

4. **You**      *Point to another person with index finger.*

5. **Girl**      *Run thumb down right side of your cheek.*

6. **Boy**      *Open and close right hand near forehead as if holding the bill of a cap.*

# TREASURE COINS

Take a look at some of the coins the children saw in the exhibit. These are real coins, and they are real old!

### Piece of Eight

*"Eight what?", Jack asked.*
*This is an eight real or eight bit coin,*
*worth a dollar when it was made. If*
*you look closely, you can see part of*
*the figure "8". This coin has been*
*cut. When someone needed to give*
*another person part of a dollar, they*
*could actually cut a piece off of the coin. This coin has*
*about 60 cents left on it.*

### Spanish Cobs

*These handmade*
*coins were weighed*
*very carefully and*
*the demonination,*
*mint, assayer,*
*date, and Spanish*
*designs were hand*
*hammered on to*
*them. These coins*
*are 8 reales, 4*

*reales, 2 reals, 1 real, and 1/2 real. 8 reales is a dollar, 4 reales*
*is 50 cents, 2 reales is 25 cents, 1 real is 12.5 cents, and a half*
*real is worth 6.25 cents. These coins were made in the 1600s*
*and 1700s.*

### Knight Rider
*This is a Dutch Colonial Daalder, a silver dollar, from the shipwreck of "The Love". This coin was made in 1711 in Holland.*

### Gold Doubloon
*This is the front and back view of a 1791 4 escudo gold doubloon. This coin was found in a farm field after the crop was harvested.*

### 1776 Silver Dollar
*This 8 real coin was made in 1776 in Mexico. It is a Spanish coin, as Spain controlled the Mexican mines at that time.*

*The coins shown on the previous pages as well as on the cover of this book are courtesy of Treasures of Maryland. If you wish to learn more about Spanish Colonial coins, visit your local library, search for information online, or contact:*

**Treasures of Maryland**
PO Box 1275
Salisbury, Maryland  21802

treasuresofmaryland@comcast.net

# NOTES

# NOTES

SHEEPDOG PRESS

"Woof!"